CHRISTMAS IN MY HEART

CHRISTMAS IN MY HEART

Joe L. Wheeler

REVIEW AND HERALD® PUBLISHING ASSOCIATION
HAGERSTOWN, MD 21740

This book was
Edited by Raymond H. Woolsey
Designed by Bill Kirstein
Cover Design: Helcio Deslandes
Cover art: Superstock/Currier & Ives
Type set: Goudy Old Style

PRINTED IN U.S.A.

96 95 94   10 9 8 7 6 5 4

Library of Congress Cataloging in Publication Data

Christmas in my heart / [compiled by] Joe L. Wheeler.
        p. cm.

    1. Christmas stories, American. I. Wheeler, Joe L., 1936–
PS648.C45C447   1992
813'.010833—dc20
                                            92-27484
                                                CIP

ISBN 0-8280-0672-5

Acknowledgments

"Introduction: Once Upon a Christmas," by Joe L. Wheeler. Copyright 1992. Printed by permission of the author.

"The Snow of Christmas," by Joe L. Wheeler. Written in 1989. Printed by permission of the author.

"Christmas Is for Families," by Lois Hansen. Originally published in *The Youth's Instructor*, Dec. 16, 1958. Reprinted by permission of the author.

"Christmas Echoes" by Les Thomas. Originally published in (Fort Worth) *Star-Telegram*, Dec. 25, 1976. Reprinted by permission of the (Fort Worth) *Star-Telegram*.

"*A Certain Small Shepherd*," by Rebecca Caudill. Copyright © 1965 by Rebecca Caudill. Reprinted by permission of Henry Holt and Company, Inc.

"A String of Blue Beads," from *A String of Blue Beads*, by Fulton Oursler. Copyright 1951 by Reader's Digest Association, Inc. Used by permission of Doubleday, a division of Bantam Doubleday Dell Publishing Group, Inc.

"The Red Mittens," by Hartley F. Dailey. Originally published in *Sunshine*, Dec. 1961. Reprinted by permission of the author.

"David's Star of Bethlehem," by Christine Whiting Parmenter. From the book *Stories of Courage and Devotion*, by Christine Whiting Parmenter. Copyright © 1939, 1967. Used by permission of the publisher, Julian Messner, a division of Simon & Schuster, New York.

"The Promise of the Doll" by Ruth C. Ikerman. Originally published by *Christian Herald*. Reprinted by permission of *Christian Herald*.

"The Christmas of the Phonograph Records," by Mari Sandoz. Originally published in *Sandhill Sundays and Other Recollections*, by Mari Sandoz (University of Nebraska Press, 1970). Copyright © 1966 by the Estate of Mari Sandoz. Reprinted by permission of McIntosh and Otis, Inc.

"Bethany's Christmas Carol" by Mabel McKee. Originally published in McKee's *The Golden Thread* (Fleming H. Revell Company). Reprinted by permission of Fleming H. Revell Company, Gleneida Publishing Group.

"A Few Bars in the Key of G." Author and original source unknown. If anyone can provide knowledge of origins of this old story, please relay information to Joe L. Wheeler, care of Review and Herald Publishing Association.

"Guest in the House," by Ruth Emery Amanrude. Originally published in *Christian Herald*. Reprinted by permission of *Christian Herald*.

"Gift for David," by Lon Woodrum. Originally published in *The War Cry*, Dec. 1958. Reprinted by permission of The Salvation Army and *The War Cry*.

"Why the Minister Did Not Resign." Author and original source unknown. If anyone can provide knowledge of origins of this old story, please relay information to Joe L. Wheeler, care of Review and Herald Publishing Association.

"The Why of Christmas," by Don Dedera. Written in 1967. Printed by permission of the author.

" 'Meditation' in a Minor Key," by Joe L. Wheeler. Written in 1991. Printed by permission of the author.

Contents

DECEMBER

MERRIE XMAS

Once Upon a Christmas . . .

"ONCE upon a time . . ." Any self-respecting fairy tale begins there. Fairy tales, born as they are in the folk-consciousness of a race, deal, not with externals, but with the basics, with the well-springs of our thoughts and actions. The same is true of the Christmas story. The good ones, the ones that refuse to die, are almost primitive in their simplicity and lack of subterfuge. And they are unabashedly sentimental.

Of all the times in the year when sentiment prevails, none exceeds Christmas. Undoubtedly, the time of year helps. The nights are long, the air is cold and tangy, snow flocks city and county streets with ermine, the pace of life slows just a little, and the low temperatures cause us to be more aware of the presence or absence of human warmth, in whatever form it may manifest itself. It's hard to imagine us singing Christmas carols in 100° July, for instance. So, somehow, nature, tradition, and just plain luck joined forces to bring us this most special of all days at just the right time of year.

Christmas is family time. Thus, at no time in the year are refugees from death or separation more likely to be racked by waves of loneliness—and let's face it, if you were to choose just one word to symbolize the essence of America in the last decade of the century, it would have to be the word "lonely."

We are a most lonely race—and we are getting lonelier. We try to wall out the realization of just how lonely we are by all sorts of artificial barricades: noise, TV, radio, talk, movies, videos, activity, liquor, drugs, sports—and most of the year we succeed fairly well. All except at Christmas. For some reason, the normal defenses don't work at Christmas. When you can't go home at Christmas you realize just how dead-end and lacking in substance or meaning your life is—a graphic case in point, the high suicide rate during or just after the holidays.

One of the greatest tragedies of our time is the shattering of the family unit. Without a solid family system no nation has ever flourished long on this planet. Belatedly, we are discovering that television and other mass media have replaced the family and God as the focal center of our society. When Christless programming of the child's ethical computers takes the place of God and value-centered home and church programming, it is a foregone conclusion that the result is a lost generation. No more lost generation have we ever known.

But all is not lost. And one of the solutions to our dilemma is to rediscover the enduring "once upon a Christmas" values, recognizing that a society divorced from God—or a family divorced from God—can do nothing but self-destruct.

Again, we come back to sentiment. One can no more truly experience Christmas in all its dimensions without emotion than one can fall in love on a completely rational plane. Part of the loveliness of Christmas lies in this melodious interplay of love, caring, laughter, tears, forgiveness, empathy, healing, etc., among the strings of our souls. Unfortunately, much of the literature of Christmas is sterile, lacking the awesome power of great Christmas stories: the power to make you laugh or cry, the power to uplift your spirit, the power to radically change your behavior patterns so that you may begin a new life.

Non-Christians cannot write great Christmas stories; they frequently try, but they are as ephemeral and transitory as cascading autumn leaves. These writers fail to notice one great truth: without the God-induced love for one's fellow-creatures, Christmas is no more than a Madison Avenue after-Thanksgiving sale.

One of the earliest and fondest memories of my childhood has to do with these stories that touch the heart. Often I wing my way back through time by replaying one of these mental videos: the *real* tree, the *real* caring, the *real* people, the *real* relationships with man and God that these "once upon a Christmas" stories revealed.

And when I see these scenes flash on the screen again, almost invariably . . . there she is: Mother. An elocutionist of the old school, Mother knew the great stories almost by heart. Those great ones that never grew old, no matter how many times we had heard them before. We knew them practically by heart ourselves: we knew when the laugh parts were nearing . . . and we knew by Mother's slowing pace that she was going to cry. It was stories like these that painted individual Christmas canvases with such vivid colors. So timeless and precious are these stories that no sacrifice is too much, no cost too great, to pay . . . in order to go "home for Christmas" and hear those cathartic stories once again. They give love, family, home, and God meaning . . . focus.

How This Collection Came to Be

For some three decades I have been gathering some very special stories of Christmas. For a number of years I made copies of the stories and gave them out to friends at Christmas time. The response was overwhelming. In turn, these friends have helped me find more of these elusive stories that are disappearing at an alarming rate.

Unquestionably, the Golden Age of Christmas Stories occurred during the first third of this century; actually, it began in the 1890s and receded during the 1940s. Evidently, this was a period of spiritual renewal in America . . . and, not surprisingly, it parallels the Social Gospel Period (which was born with Charles Sheldon's *In His Steps* in 1898 and flowered with Harold Bell Wright's trilogy: *That Printer of Udel's*, *The Calling of Dan Matthews*, and *God and the Groceryman*, as well as in the writings of a number of other authors who had a deep conviction that the essence of Christianity is not sterile doctrine but the application of Biblical principles into a caring relationship with all those who we contact on a daily basis).

But even though the churning out of these stories slowed to a comparable trickle after mid-century, it never completely stopped. They continue to be written today. It is my conviction—supported by students of our society—that America is returning to the values represented by these stories. Everywhere we see a renewed interest in one's roots, one's family. During the holidays we see families making greater attempts to get together again. Paradoxically, in an age where one out of every two marriages ends in divorce, we see an almost feverish attempt to corral the few shreds of family that remain.

Which brings us to orphans. Interestingly enough, a surprisingly large number of the memorable Christmas stories deal with orphans. Today, orphans in the traditional sense are vastly outnumbered by those "orphans" who are deprived of adult love and protection by divorce. Let's face it: the results are almost indistinguishable. In fact, it oft appears that the latter may be *more* traumatic—no matter what the age—than physical death.

I am reminded of one of the most moving open letters I have ever read, a letter that was addressed to the editor of a large metropolitan newspaper. The writer was a middle-aged woman whose senior-citizen parents had recently divorced, the father having found someone younger and more attractive.

The writer observed that the resulting loss of focus came home to roost every Christmas because there was no longer any home to go to. Mom was alone, embittered and impoverished, in a small apartment; Dad and his new live-in represented a totally alien world, a world that the daughter and family felt was antithetical to their values. So utterly lost did she feel, in a moral sense, that she found herself (even at that age) floundering in a sea of doubt, unable to find bedrock anywhere.

At this juncture, I feel it would be good for us to observe an important point: there is a crucial difference between Christmas stories that merely entertain and those that touch the heart. I have seen a number of anthologies of Christmas stories for sale, and bought them—on the strength of the title or reviews, all of which trumpeted the news that they were "great" Christmas stories—only to discover that the bulk (if not all) of them, although technically well-written and featuring some of the most famous author names of our age, lacked that one ingredient I consider absolutely essential: that the story touch the heart itself. Without this intangible variable I personally refuse to grant an accolade such as "great" to any story, no matter how much of a high-flyer the author is and no matter how well written the story may be literarily.

The other side of the coin is the fact that, from a purely technical point of view, a number of the stories I have included in this treasury are flawed. Nevertheless, I included them because of their emotive and convicting power.

My Dream

It is my hope that this collection of stories (culled from hundreds) will represent more than shelf fodder to you, that the characters in these stories will become old friends—to be taken down and shared with your family and friends every Christmas season. I included only those stories that I have shared with others enough to be certain of their power.

Most important of all, however, in motivating me to finally, after all these years, take the time to select the pure gold of the collection for publication, was the conviction that there is such a great need today for Christ-centered Christmas stories that will remind us, every time we read one, that this is really what Christmas—and life itself—is all about. Without it, Christmas is but a hollow drum beaten by commercial opportunists, or to paraphrase Shakespeare: "a tale told by an idiot, full of sophistry and futility, signifying *nothing*."

I have taken occasional editorial liberties: up-dating words or terms that have become archaic or have acquired negative connotations.

Welcome to the timeless world of Christmas.

Coda

Each reader of this collection can make a difference. If enough readers respond positively to the collection and communicate your reactions to me, we will consider putting together a second collection of stories—there are so many splendid ones I had to leave out! (And, if you know the earliest origin or true authorship of a story we have not been able to track to its source, please relay that to us so we can correct it before another printing.) Furthermore, I am positive that some of the greatest stories haven't even been found yet; thus I hope that each of you will search for them and take the time to send me copies of the best ones for possible inclusion in the next collection (be sure to include author, publisher, and date, if possible).

Joe L. Wheeler, Ph.D.
c/o Review and Herald
55 W. Oak Ridge Drive
Hagerstown, MD 21740

The Snow of Christmas

Joe Lawrence Wheeler

How is a story born? I don't know; it just comes to you. One bitterly cold December evening in 1989, when I had just turned in grades for my creative writing class, the mood came upon me to write a Christmas story of my own.

Misunderstandings—every marriage is full of them. But what happens when they are permitted to grow unchecked? What then? We all know the answer: another divorce. As I looked out at the snow and ice on the river, and heard the cold wind shriek as it savaged the trees, there was born the story of a great love destroyed by a quarrel.

I sent out copies to friends. So many wrote back, thanking me and encouraging me to print it, that it proved the catalyst for pulling this collection together.

John, Cathy, and Julie—and then there were only two.

THREE doors he had slammed on her: the bedroom, the front, and the car. What started it all, he really couldn't say; it was just one of those misunderstandings that grow into quarrels. In a matter of minutes he had unraveled a relationship that had taken years to build. His tongue, out of control, appeared to have a life of its own, divorced as it was from his accusing mind and withdrawing heart.

"Catherine . . . It's all been a big mistake . . . you and me. I've tried and tried—Heaven knows I've tried—but it just won't work. You're . . . you're wrong for me . . . and I'm wrong for you."

"John!"

"Don't interrupt me. I mean it. We're through. What we thought was love, wasn't. It just wasn't . . . No sense in prolonging a dead thing. Don't worry, I'll see to it that you don't suffer financially—I'll keep making the house payments. . . . And uh . . . and uh, you can keep what's in the checking and savings accounts. . . . And uh, uh, don't worry, I'll send child support for Julie!"

"John!"

Almost, he came to his senses as he looked into Catherine's anguished eyes and saw the shock and the tears. But his pride was at stake; ignoring the wounded appeal of those azure eyes, he had stormed out, his leaving punctuated by the three slammed doors.

Three weeks later, here he was, pacing a lonely motel room 3,000 miles from home. Home? He had no home. He had only his job—a very good one—and his Mercedes. That was all.

Unable to face the prosecuting attorney of his mind, he turned on the TV, but that didn't help much. There were Christmas-related commercials or programs on every channel—one of these ads featured a golden-haired little girl who reminded him far too much of Julie.

He remembered Julie's wide-eyed anticipation of every Christmas. The presents under the tree that she'd surreptitiously pick up and evaluate by weight and size and sound, and the finesse with which she unwrapped and rewrapped them . . . ; he found it hard to be stern with her for did not Catherine too unwrap them on the sly? It seemed that Catherine had been constitutionally unable to wait until Christmas should reveal what hid within gaily-wrapped packages bearing her name, so poor Julie came about this affliction naturally.

Again, he switched channels. Wouldn't you know it—yet another Christmas special. Had to be Perry Como . . . *Still* at it. Why, the Christmas special advertised as Como's farewell performance was a number of years back—in fact, he and Catherine heard it the Christmas season of Julie's birth . . . Como no longer had the range, but his middle tones still carried him through.

Oh no! Not "I'll Be Home for Christmas" . . . "you can plan on me . . ." On the wings of Como's voice he soared backward in time, all the way back to his own childhood.

Was it his seventh Christmas, or his eighth? "The eighth!" . . . for that was the year his parents had surprised him with an adorable shaded-silver Persian kitten, which he promptly named "Samantha." Samantha had lived a long time—15 years, in fact. It was hard to envision life without that bundle of purring fur that cuddled up next to his feet every night until he left for college. And even then, whenever he returned home, every night, like clockwork, within 60 seconds from when he turned out the light and slipped into bed, he would sense a slight vibration resulting from a four-point landing; he would hear a loud purr, and feel a whiskered head searching for a head-scratching.

Memories flooded in upon him in torrents now. How he had loved Christmas at home. His had always been the responsibility of decorating the Christmas tree—a tree he got to pick out himself. A *real* tree, never a fake! The fragrance of a real tree, the sticky feel of a real tree, even the shedding of a real tree, were all intertwined in the memories of the years.

Strange . . . passing strange . . . how he measured the years by specific Christmases.

The Christmas of the "Broken Phonograph Records," with its now legendary "lean-to" by . . . uh . . . Mari Sandoz—yeah, Sandoz wrote it. How everyone had laughed and cried over that Nebraska frontier tale. "Lean-to" had gone into the family lexicon of memories. And, as usual, all four of his grandparents had been there, and numerous aunts, uncles, cousins, and family friends.

Then there was the Christmas when Dad, for the first time, read *all* of Dickens' "Christmas Carol"—he had thought it would never end. But strangely, ever since that first reading, the story of Scrooge and the Cratchits seemed shorter every time it was read. And theater and movie renditions? They but reinforced the impact of the core story.

And how could he ever forget the first time he had heard Henry Van Dyke's "The Other Wise Man"? Like Dickens' tale, it normally took several evenings to read. That poignant conclusion where the dying Artaban, under the extended shadow of Golgotha, at last finds his king—it never failed to bring tears to his eyes.

"That's *enough*, John! You've got to put all that behind you. Christmas? What is it but Madison Avenue's annual process of grafting sales to sentiment? That's why the first Christmas sale now takes place the day after Independence Day." But it wasn't enough: he just could not convince himself that Christmas meant no more than that. Instead, his mind flung open a door and replayed the scene in his parents' kitchen three weeks before.

It had been anything but easy—rather, it had been perhaps the hardest thing he had ever done, telling them about the separation and impending divorce. And he had begged off from being home for this Christmas, telling them that a very important business meeting on the East Coast would make it impossible.

Mother had broken down when she heard about the end of his marriage, for Catherine had slipped into their hearts, becoming the daughter they had always yearned for, that first Christmas when he brought her home from college. Catherine had taken it all in: the warmth and radiance of the *real* tree; the crudely carved nativity scene (John had made it when he was 12); the exterior Christmas lights; the Christmas decorations everywhere; the Christmas music played on the stereo and sung around the piano; the Christmas stories read during the week; the puns, jokes, kidding, and ever-present laughter; the crazy annual trading game—which was more fun than the usual exchange of presents; the bounteous table groaning with delicious food day after day; parlor games such as Monopoly, caroms, dominoes, anagrams; the crackling fire every evening; the remembering of the Christ Child; and the warmth and love that permeated every corner of the modest home.

When he had proposed—on Christmas Eve—and apologized for the plainness of the home, and compared it to the Marin County estate where she grew up, her eyes had blazed and she had hushed his lips with her fingers.

"Don't you *ever* apologize for your home, John!" she exclaimed. "There is *love* here, and Christ, and Father, *and* Mother—not just my lonely embittered father rattling around in all those endless rooms, *alone*. No, this,"... she paused as her gaze took it all in again... "this is the kind of home I've longed for all my life." Then her eyes, reflecting the firelight glow, softened and emanated such tender, trusting love—unqualified and unreserved—that time stopped for him as he gathered into his arms what had once seemed virtually unattainable.

"This has got to stop!" he admonished himself. "There can be no turning back!" Out of the room he strode, down the hall, down the stairs, and out into the city. The streets were crowded with people—it was December 23—all with one goal: get those last-minute gifts. He passed two Salvation Army bell ringers, and left a five-dollar bill with each one.

Happiness and seasonal good humor were all around him. Strangers wished him a very merry Christmas. Christmas carols were piped into almost every store.

His attention was caught by a crowd in front of Macy's biggest window; he pushed himself far enough in to be able to see what they were all looking at. What he saw, in a fairyland setting, were hundreds of cashmere teddy bears in varying costumes. Julie had fallen in love with them the first time she saw them (long before they had become the rage of the season). And he had planned to surprise her on Christmas morning by bringing it to her at the breakfast table rather than putting it under the tree. Oh well, perhaps Catherine would remember to buy it, that is—

which he rather doubted—if she was in the mood to have Christmas at all.

He moved on, but seemed to feel an invisible force pulling him back to Macy's. Two hours later, unable to resist any longer, he went back, bought one of the last three in stock—even the window had been cleaned out—and returned to the motel. He shook his head, not understanding in the least why he had bought it, for he was a continent away from Julie—and tomorrow was Christmas Eve.

After depositing the teddy bear in his room, he returned to the street. This time, he walked away from the downtown district. He came to a large white New England-style church. The front doors were open, and floating out on the night air were the celestial strains of "Ave Maria." He stopped, transfixed; then he walked up the steps and into the church. There, down candle-lit aisles, at the front of the church, was a live nativity scene. Off to the side, a lovely brunette, eyes luminous with the illusion of the moment, was singing the same song he had first heard Catherine sing, and with the same intensity, forgetfulness of self, and sincerity.

When she reached those last few measures and her pure voice seemed to commingle with the angels, chills went up and down his spine; when the last note died away into infinity, there came the ultimate accolade of total silence . . . followed by a storm of applause.

John closed his eyes, soothed yet tormented by

what he had just experienced, by whom the singer reminded him of, and by the significance of that mother's love and sacrifice 2,000 years ago.

Out of the sanctuary he strode, and down the street, mile after mile, until he had left even the residential district behind. On and on he walked; he did not stop until the city lights no longer kept him from seeing the stars. As he looked up into the cold December sky, for the first time in three traumatic weeks he faced his inner self.

And he did not like what he saw.

Etched for all time in the grooves of his memory were the terrible words he had spoken to the woman he had pledged his life to. How could he have been so cruel—even if he no longer loved her? That brought him face to face with the rest of his life. The question, the answer, and what he would do about it, would, one way or another, dramatically affect every member of his immediate family, from now and until the day they died.

What was his answer to be?

* * * * *

It was snowing! For the first time in 10 years, declared the radio announcer, there would be snow on Christmas. The windshield wipers kept time with Bing Crosby, who comes back to life every December just to sing "I'm Dreaming of a White Christmas." The lump in his throat was almost more than he could handle. Would this be a Christmas "just like the ones I used to know"? Could she—*would* she—consider taking him back?

Although bone-weary from staying up all night and from the frantic search for airline reservations, he was far too tense to be sleepy. The flight had been a noisy one, and a colicky baby right behind him had ensured a wide-awake trip. He'd rented a car, and now . . . his heart pounded louder as each mile slipped past on the odometer.

Now that he had thrown away the most precious things in life—his wife and child—he no longer even had a home. Belatedly, he realized that without that, life's skies for him would lose their blue. How odd that his mind meshed the graying of his personal skies with the cold-graying of Cathy's eyes when he mentioned divorce: the blue of both was now as silvery as the ice- and snow-bedecked trees that flashed by.

The road became icier and he narrowly averted an accident several times. Occasionally a vehicle would spin out of control in front of him, but somehow he got around them safely.

At last! The city limits. He could hardly keep his runaway heart from jumping its tracks.

Had the road to his house ever seemed so long? Then he turned that last corner . . . Darkness: no lights, no car! He fought panic as he skidded into the driveway, got out, and fought the bitterly cold wind and snow to the back door. Inside, all appeared normal—nothing to indicate that Cathy and Julie had left on a long trip.

Maybe they were at his parents' house! He rushed

back to the car, backed out onto the street, and sped out of town, hoping against hope that he was guessing right. He didn't dare to trust his fate to a telephone call.

About an hour later he saw the cheery lights of his folks' place. Through the front window he could see the multicolored lights on the Christmas tree. And *there*, in the driveway, was his wife's car.

He passed the house, then circled back on an alley road, cutting his lights as he reapproached the house. His heart now thumping like a jackhammer, he brushed off his clothes and shoes and ever so quietly opened the back door and stepped into the gloom of the dark hall.

He heard a child's voice, singing. He edged around the corner into the foyer. Kerosene lamps, as always, gave to the room a dreamy serenity. His folks sat on the couch intensely watching their grandchild as she softly sang, kneeling by his nativity stable:
"Silent night, holy night,
  All is calm, all is bright; . . ."
There was a look of ethereal beauty about her, lost as she was in her Bethlehem world.

"Oh, God," he prayed, "shield her from trouble, from pain—from growing up too soon."

Then, like a sword thrust through his chest, came the realization that he—her own father—had thrust her out of that protected world that children need so desperately if they are to retain their illusions, that child-like trust without which none of us will ever reach heaven's gate.

The sweet but slightly wobbly voice continued, then died away with the almost whispered
"Jesus, Lord, at Thy birth,
  Jesus, Lord, at Thy birth."

His heart wrenched as he drank in every inch of that frail flowering of the love he and Cathy had planted. Oh, how little it would take to blight that fragile blossom!

He wondered what his daughter had been told. . . . Would she still love him? Would she ever again trust him completely?

Upon completion of the beloved Schubert hymn, Julie sank down to the level of the nativity figures and, propping her head on her elbows, gazed fixedly into another time.

John now turned to an older version of Julie; this one leaned against the window frame. She was wearing a rose-colored gown that, in the flickering light from the oak logs in the fireplace, revealed rare beauty of face and form. But her face—such total desolation John had never seen before. In all the years that followed, that image of suffering was so indelibly burned into his memory that he was never able to bury it in his subconscious.

How woebegone, how utterly weary, she appeared. A lone tear glistened as it trickled down that cheek he had loved to kiss.

Oh, how he loved her!

He could hold back no longer. Silently, he approached her. Was it too late?

Suddenly, she sensed his presence and turned away from the vista of falling snow to look at him. She delayed the moment of reckoning by initially refusing to meet his eyes . . . then, very slowly, she raised her wounded eyes to his . . . and searched for an answer.

Oh, the relief that flooded over him when he saw her eyes widen as they were engulfed by the tidal wave of love that thundered across the five-foot abyss between them. In fact, it was so overwhelming that neither could ever remember how the distance was bridged—only that, through his tears, he kept saying, as he crushed her to him, "Oh, Cathy! Oh, Cathy! Forgive me, Cathy. Oh, Cathy, I love you so!"

And then there were three at the window—not counting the snow-coated teddy bear—the rest of the world forgotten in the regained heaven of their own.

And the snow of Christmas Eve continued to fall.

Christmas Is for Families

Lois Hansen

How often we needlessly worry about furnishings in a house, as we anticipate the arrival of company we have to impress, only to discover that the love manifested in the home creates a magic mist that gilds everything far more than any number of priceless antiques ever could have. This particular story—written by a cherished friend of our family—has long been a favorite of ours for it portrays just such a—not a house, but a home.

MARTHA Dean wrestled with her problem all during the confusion that was the usual family breakfast.

As she toasted and stirred and fried to please each individual taste, she was only partly conscious of the family talk that rolled on about her. Her mind was far away, and yet so automatic had this early morning task become that her busy hands moved of their own accord, leaving her mind free to work on all angles of her bothersome problem.

At last the minor crises had all been solved. Her husband, Jim, had found his lost letter, Jimmie was assured that he really must wear his raincoat, and a stamp was magically produced for Jill. Jimmie was the last to go, and as the door banged shut behind his hurrying feet, Martha lifted baby Petey into his high-chair and began to spoon cereal into his open mouth.

Petey looked at his mother and chuckled as though it was all very funny.

Martha smiled back at her youngest son, but worriedly. "It's really no joke, son. I don't know what to do. The problem seems to get bigger all the time. If your big brother Larry hadn't married a girl who has always had everything, maybe I wouldn't take it so hard. But with all Fran has been used to, how can I ask her and Larry to come and visit in this old house? And yet, if Larry doesn't come home for Christmas—"

Martha paused. There was Jill, too. Maybe it was a blessing in disguise that her boy friend, Bob, wanted her to come up to his folks' cabin for the skiing. He might fall out of love with her if he saw how her family lived.

Martha looked at the pile of breakfast dishes and winced a little.

"Come on, Petey," she said with sudden decision. "Let's go on a tour of this monstrosity and see if anything can be done in the next few weeks to turn the place into a dream house, so I can feel up to inviting my sophisticated older children and their wealthy partners home for Christmas."

"Cwistmas," Petey gurgled as his mother buttoned him into a red sweater and went out into the fresh morning air.

Martha walked along the old-fashioned brick walk.

I needn't be ashamed of my garden anyway, she thought.

The rich purple of the cinerias and primroses made a lovely frame for the green of the lawn. A few new blossoms were appearing on the stocks, and the poinsettia bush made a charming picture against the white wall.

If we could just be like Adam and Eve and have gardens without houses, Martha thought.

She turned at the gate and tried to pretend that she was seeing the house through Fran's and Bob's eyes. They were, after all, the ones who would notice its shabby appearance most. Larry and Jill had grown up here. They knew the old place by heart. But of course they might see its shabbiness in an entirely new light, now that they had become familiar with such lovely homes.

Martha's gray eyes traveled over the object of her concern. No. It would never do. The great sprawling mass was of no particular period. The upper story sat primly in the center of the roof like a spinster's best hat. The many windows were high and small. *Something like those old-fashioned glasses my Uncle George used to wear.* She smiled in remembrance.

The white paint glistened in occasional spurts of sunshine and the front screen door was tipped at a rather rakish angle, as if it had been slammed too often and too hard by little people who were in a real hurry to get outside.

And that backyard. Martha closed her eyes and wished she could as easily dispose of the backyard problem. But the sweet peas planted against the side of the garage would be lovely in the spring and would help to soften the picture.

Just in time, Petey was rescued from a puddle left by the recent rain. His hand nestled warmly into Martha's as she said, "Let's go upstairs, Pete, and see the ocean, and in the meantime try to discover some magic to turn those worn old bedrooms into some like they have in magazine pictures."

On the upstairs landing they paused for a moment, and Martha caught her breath at the wealth of beauty spread all about her. "This particular stretch of the Pacific Ocean must be the loveliest place in the whole world," she said to herself.

The lacy branches of the eucalyptus trees at the edge of the lagoon made patterns against the gray of the sky, and farther out against the edge of the cliff the ocean sprawled and rolled, sending its fountains of spray high in the air.

Turning into the narrow hall, Martha opened each door in turn, and shut it again almost as quickly.

Jim's long sick spell and the trip East for Larry's wedding, coming so close together, had taken all they had saved for remodeling these rooms.

Downstairs again, Martha tied on her old apron and mentally counted her blessings as she started the breakfast dishes at last.

"I guess a person can't have everything, and Jim's being well is worth more than a whole tract of houses."

That night Martha talked the problem over with Jim.

"If I could just have new curtains for the living room," she sighed. "These give the outside of the house such a forlorn look."

"I know, honey, and I wish you could, too," he answered. "But everything seems to come due at Christmas—taxes, insurance—everything. This year we have Jill's trip to manage, too. Maybe next year."

Martha nodded. "I suppose so. But it would be so wonderful to have the house fixed up and all the children under the same roof again."

"Fathers have their lonesome moments, too," Jim answered. "Maybe I don't always say very much, but I remember well enough when Larry and Jill were small, and wish it could be that way this year. But honey, if we do have them come, it will have to be with the house just as it is."

* * * * *

In the weeks that followed, Christmas trees began to appear on the street corners. Lights began to glow in the store windows, parents went shopping with eager little boys and girls, and even the old house took on a festive air.

Wreaths hung in the downstairs windows, and the big tree that Jim and Jimmie brought in from the hills glowed with lights and wore its ancient ornaments proudly.

The big kitchen began to come alive with the sounds and smells of Christmas. Everyone helped crack the nuts for the cookies and fruitcake Martha sent to Fran and Larry. Jars were filled with nuts and candies for gifts. The recipes Martha's grandmother had used were used again.

Petey got in everyone's way and was hugged and kissed a hundred times a day. Snatches of carols floated out of the house as Jill taught the two little boys the same old songs she and Larry had learned, meanwhile walking on a rosy cloud as the days grew fewer and fewer till she would see her Bob again.

The day before Christmas, the gift came from Fran and Larry. Martha's heart turned over as she took the wrappings off a magnificent picture of Jesus and His disciples on the way to Emmaus.

"Oh, Mother!" Jill gasped.

"Sa-a-ay! That's all right," Jim said, admiring the painting.

"Where'll we hang it, Mom?" the always practical Jimmie wondered.

Petey just chuckled as he wrapped the tissue from the box around his head and urged everyone to play peeka-boo.

"Did you know about this, Jill?" Martha asked, with a knowing glance.

"No, I didn't, Mother, but isn't it beautiful?"

"It's what I've always wanted," Martha sighed happily. "Wasn't it sweet of them. And yet," her eyes were wistful, "I wish they could be here to enjoy it with us."

"Hey!" Jim shouted, with a quick glance at the clock. "Was someone supposed to catch a train? Look at the time, Jill!"

"Oh, Dad, Bob would have a fit if I missed it. We had planned to stay with his folks tonight and go on to Tahoe with the crowd tomorrow."

"Sounds like fun," Martha said on the way to the station. "We'll miss our girl on Christmas, but judging from the stars in your eyes, your Christmas will be a very happy one."

The house was quiet after Jill had left. Martha and Jim read the old, loved Christmas stories to the little boys and helped them hang up the all-important Christmas stockings. And when the family were all in bed,

Martha shed a few quick tears as she said a special prayer for the ones who weren't home this Christmas Eve.

The sound of bells awakened them on Christmas morning. Martha lay quietly listening to their message, before a shout from the living room brought her to her feet. Jimmie had found his Erector set and Petey was running his new wagon around and around, finding a few new places to scratch on the shabby furniture.

After breakfast, Jim took the boys to the beach and Martha cleared out mountains of tissue, trying not to feel sorry for herself. The activities involved in getting Christmas dinner for three hungry people kept her mind off her lonesomeness.

The little boys returned from the beach, and, tired from their play, took a nap before dinner. Jim sat in the sudden quiet, reading the news magazines he scarcely had time to see on work days.

"Peace—it's wonderful," Jim grinned at Martha as she stole time from her cooking for a small rest on his lap and a Christmas kiss.

"Doesn't the house look nice, dear? Christmas things hide a lot, and no one will ever see the scratches anymore. They won't have eyes for anything but our beautiful picture." Martha's glance lingered possessively on the scene as she spoke.

"Like it, Mommy?" Jim asked. "I thought the card that came with it was a beauty, too."

"It was. But you know what I wish, don't you, Jim?"

"Of course I do! You, my dear, are incurably a mother, and if your chicks aren't with you, your feathers droop."

The table was delightful with Jill's centerpiece of a fat red candle and Christmas greens. The beautifully ironed linen cloth was an old one that had worn thin in the 25 years since Martha had been a bride. And Jimmie had polished the old silver until the satiny finish reflected the soft candle glow.

The crisp brown of the nut loaf flanked by the tiny creamed onions and a mound of fluffy mashed potatoes, along with home-canned pickles and Martha's own special fruit salad, caused Jim to heave a great hungry sigh as he buckled Petey into his high chair and sat down at the head of the table.

"Enough food here for an army, dear. You are going to have to remember that your family is getting smaller all the time."

Martha smiled, and glanced around the table to be sure everything was in order. She was glad that Jimmie had washed his hands and face without being told.

The little boys bowed their heads, and their father's deep voice asked God to "Bless our food, and those who are not with us, and keep them safe today."

And when the amen was said, Petey's ready smile broke through the moment of longing as he reached out both fat hands for the "Tatoes, pease!"

"Jim, did that sound like a car to you?" Martha paused in the act of filling Petey's plate.

"I didn't hear anything," Jim answered. "Jimmie, do you want to go and see?"

Jimmie's eyes were like saucers in his round freckled face as he rushed back from his trip to the front door.

"Daddy! Mother! They're all here!"

Martha had half risen from her place, but it was Jim who spoke. "Who, son?"

"Jill and Larry and Fran, and that guy Jill went to see." But Martha was halfway to the front door, and Larry's eager arms were around his mother's waist, with Fran close beside.

As Martha turned to Jill the girl said shyly, "This is Bob, Mother." Martha's eyes liked what they saw.

Jim had never looked so happy as when his tall son slapped his shoulder and told him how glad they were to be home.

Jimmy danced about like a wild Indian, and only his mother's reproving glance kept him from uttering an original war cry. Petey ran to get his new red wagon and bring it to Fran for her approval.

The dinner was marvelous, the children said, and

Fran seemed to enjoy it most of all. Jimmie and Bob found a common interest in model planes, and Jimmie had another hero besides Larry.

The big log crackled in the fireplace after the dishes were done, and then Martha and Jim heard the whole story.

"It all began with Jill," Larry said. "She wrote us after Thanksgiving and told us why Mother didn't feel like she could ask us to come home Christmas."

"Oh, Jill!" Martha said faintly, and blushed to the roots of her graying hair.

"Well, of course," said Jill, "Mother was embarrassed about the old house, but I just told Fran that when she saw the warmth and love pouring out of every crack of the old place, she wouldn't even notice the shabbiness."

"That's my girl," said Bob. "Does everyone see now why I love her?"

"We know better than anyone else why, I think, Bob," Jim said after the laugh that followed Bob's impulsiveness.

"But the lovely picture!" Martha turned to Fran. "Why did you send it if you were coming?"

"Jill's letter came the day we sent the gift," Fran answered, "and Larry got plane reservations at once." Fran looked at Larry. "It took a special kind of home to give me a husband as loving and thoughtful as Larry, and I'm so glad I belong to it too."

"We're glad too," Martha said. Then she turned to Bob. "But there's another mystery. I thought you and Jill were going to Tahoe for the skiing. How do you happen to be so far from there?"

"Simple as anything. When Jill told me she had heard from Fran, and that they were coming, well, I knew she wanted to be with her family. So here we are." Bob smiled. "There will be skiing till May, but only one Christmas all year."

"Will you play for us, Mother, while we sing the carols?" Larry suggested.

"Oh, no! I can't, Larry. I don't practice anymore and I make so many mistakes. In fact, Jill told me the other day that I'm the only person she knows who can play each hand in a different key."

Everybody laughed.

"But we want you to do it just like the old days," Larry begged.

Martha played them all, from "We Three Kings" to "Jingle Bells." The old house seemed to fold them close as the young voices rose and fell in the Christmas melodies. Even Petey's baby voice shrilled out bravely in "Silent Night, Holy Night."

At last the fire in the fireplace burned low and evening prayers brought the little group close together.

Fran and Larry went up the stairs to Larry's old room, and Bob was given a room where he could hear the waves breaking on the shore and dream of the time when he and Jill would know the same happiness as Jill's parents.

* * * * *

Two o'clock in the morning. The old house was quiet again. Jim woke with a start. Martha was not beside him. He sat up. Where could she be? For 25 years he had always been able to reach out and touch her at night. Then he remembered and sank back again on his pillows. The children were all home, and Martha was probably up to her old tricks, roaming around to see if they were all right.

Upstairs, Martha stood for a moment outside the room of her son and the girl he loved. Their even breathing told her all was well.

The old bed in Bob's room creaked restlessly. "Dreaming of Jill, no doubt," Martha thought. "It would be nice to have the wedding in June."

Downstairs, Jill's dark head was turned slightly on her pillow, the hand with the watch from Bob tucked under her cheek.

Jimmie would never stay covered up, and Martha smoothed the tumbled blankets and kissed him lightly.

In his crib, Petey slept like a Christmas angel, the moonlight forming a halo about his golden head.

Martha crept quietly back to bed.

"They're almost all grown up, Mommy," Jim teased her gently. "You needn't cover them up all the rest of their lives."

Martha sighed happily. "Oh, Jim, was there ever such a lovely, lovely family? Houses don't really matter. It's the love in them that counts."

Christmas Echoes

Les Thomas

Reprint courtesy of the (Fort Worth) *Star Telegram*.

All around us in the inner labyrinths of those we meet is tragedy. Pain is universal in the human race and it seems to be an inexorable law of our planet that sooner or later great happiness is followed by great sorrow: it's almost like there is a universal scorekeeper somewhere tabulating, tabulating, tabulating. When the score gets too lop-sided—crash! The roof caves in.

In this wondrous story, Thomas creates through the veil of tears . . . a misty rainbow. It was only a moment, but some moments are worth several lifetimes.

GOOD evening and happy holidays. The temperature is 35 degrees under cloudy skies. The National Weather Service forecasts a 30 percent chance of snow tonight. It could be the first white Christmas on record here in 41 years."

The radio voice startled the old man who had been asleep in his stuffed chair by the fireplace. He coughed and rubbed his face and stared at the coals that rose and fell in half-hearted, tiny flames.

One word fixed his attention in the broadcast. Snow.

"That's always what they say," he muttered to himself. "But I don't see how it can happen. Not cold enough. I doubt it. I doubt it very much."

Still, the prospect was enough to make him stretch and get up unsteadily. He walked slowly over the bare living room floor and pulled back the drapes to look out over the lawn. Across the street, red, green, and yellow lights sparkled on the roof of the Williams' house and outlined the picture window in front of a flocked white tree. The old man could see Williams—his young daughter in his arms—and his wife finishing the last of the tree's decorations. A north wind brushed the trees and frosted up the window where he stood. The old man craned his neck to look as far as he could in both directions. There was not a trace of a snowflake.

He turned around and his gaze fell for a moment on the photograph in the silver frame on top of the piano. There were two people in the picture. One was a pleasant looking woman with brown hair who was dressed in an old fashioned heavy winter coat and high shoes. The other was a girl of about 6. In the photograph, the woman and the child were holding hands. They were standing in snow.

Brubaker was 72 years old. A long time ago he

promised himself that he would try to not think so much about the people in the photograph. But each Christmas it was a promise he never tried to keep. He walked over and sat down again and stared at the remnants of the fire. Ordinarily Brubaker disliked daydreams. It was a lesson he had learned. Bad to let the mind wander. Bad to dream. He came to accept that in a way that had changed him slowly, almost imperceptibly, in grades of lessening rage in the years that passed after he lost Emily and Julie.

Eventually, Brubaker was able to accept death. "Yes," he thought, "death is reality. It is truth." It was life that he could no longer trust. "Only a fool would believe in it," he ranted once, "and if you do, life will drive you crazy."

He came to believe those things not suddenly, but over the space of many years. With music, it was different. He gave that up almost immediately.

The day after the accident Brubaker resigned his job as band director of the high school. Later, he took a job at the mill, glad to be able to drown the melody that was his life in the cacophony of pounding hammers and forges. Out too, without remorse, went the piles of records. One day he very calmly took a hammer and smashed to bits all of the black discs that he and Emily had so carefully scrimped to buy. Then he collected all the sheet music and the manuscripts and quickly shredded them, too. It all lay in a heap — the whole sweet serenade of the 30s, all of Harry James, the Dorseys, Glenn Miller and Artie Shaw.

Two things survived the purge of music in Brubaker's life. One was Emily's piano. The other was a silver trumpet that rested in its cover on a shelf of the bedroom closet. Brubaker could not explain why he kept them. In fact, he had once tried to rid himself of them, too, but he found himself going after them later, with embarrassment, asking to buy them back. He told himself they were not really instruments capable of making music anymore, but only monuments. Silent monuments. And they were relics that no longer had souls or hearts. That part of them was finished. Never again, Brubaker decided, would they play melodies to taunt and remind him of the deception of happiness that had ended in such unbearable catastrophe.

Feeling chill, Brubaker shivered suddenly and coughed. He got up and walked into the kitchen, found the prescription bottle, and slowly drained the last drops into a teaspoon. He glanced at the kitchen clock. It was almost 9:00. "Perhaps it is not too late," he thought, "to get this refilled." Brubaker got a telephone book from the drawer, took his glasses out of the pocket of his sweater, and absent-mindedly put them on. He leafed through the pages: "Pawn shops . . . pet supplies . . . pharmacies . . . Hall's Drugs . . . Town Drugstore . . . Smith's Pharmacy."

* * * * *

Rheumatic and far past the age of normal retirement, Samuel Benjamin Smith stooped over greatly and his head bobbed when he walked. Beneath starch white hair, he wore old-fashioned bifocals that perched continually on the end of his nose and whenever anything happened out of the ordinary, Sam Smith's eyes would slowly elevate above the lenses like search beacons looking for whatever was the matter.

The beacons were on when Sam hung up the telephone. He turned around with his head bobbing and slowly began poking through the inventory along the back shelves of the druggist's room in the back of the ancient drugstore.

Out in front, Billy was sweeping away the last debris of the Christmas Eve rush when he heard Sam call him. Seventeen years old and a senior in high school, Billy was rounding out three years as an employee of Smith's Drug Store. He liked the job. Many times Sam had told him he was the best helper he ever had. Even customers said Billy was a natural for the drugstore business.

Already he had an offer of a full scholarship in science at the state college. After that, there would be pharmacy school. Who knows, he might even take over the business from Sam. Billy thought so. After all, he had a natural talent for it.

The only thing he could do as well was play the horn. He was first chair in the school stage band. He even played trumpet with a group of older guys who played weekend dances. But you can't make a living with that kind of music. Those days were gone and Billy knew it. Still, it was fun to fool around. Mentally, he thought of a difficult piece the group had been working on as he hurried off to the back of the store.

Sam was filling a small brown bottle with a syrupy mixture. "Looks like you'll have to make one last delivery," Sam said, looking up. "I want you to take this over to Ed Brubaker on Oak Street. It's the old brick house on the corner across from the depot." Sam twisted the cap on the bottle and looked slowly over the top of his glasses to study Billy, who was whistling softly the practice tune that was running through his mind. He stopped whistling when he saw Sam look up.

"Now there was a musician," Sam said, shaking his head, tapping the bottle of cough syrup. "Old Ed Brubaker when he was a young man could play with the best of them. Why, there was talk he even had an offer to go to New York with one of the big bands. They played real music in those days. Music was Ed's whole life. You never saw a happier fellow. He even got the high school band to sounding like a big orchestra. Those fellows were always giving the town a serenade. Ed saw to it there was always music. Easter, the Fourth of July . . . all the holidays, Ed always had the band right there. But the best of it, the very best, was always Christmas Eve. That was special. They'd all pile in those old cars and go up to the mountain. Everybody in town used to wait up to hear it. Just before midnight, Ed would raise up that trumpet and then he'd start to play, real low at first, so low you thought you were dreaming it, and then it'd get louder. Lord, it was music so sweet you'd have bet it was Gabriel himself calling you.

"And then they'd fire off that old cannon from

the school, right at the stroke of midnight. And that was how it happened. Let's see, it was Christmas 1933, no, 1934. Terrible thing. Maybe it was the cold and the snow that caused it. They never did know. That cannon just blew up in their faces. Ed was the only one who wasn't hurt. The explosion killed three people. One was a girl from the high school. The others were Ed's wife and his little daughter. It was a terrible thing to happen. Just terrible. Afterward, Ed barely said a word again to anybody, even after all these years. And he never played music again."

* * * * *

Outside, Billy shivered in the chilly wind and climbed on the delivery bicycle to ride the four blocks and make his delivery. On the way, he thought about the things Sam told him about the man who was waiting for the package in his pocket. He made the block through the business section in front of stores still crowded with late shoppers and cut down through residential streets in the old part of town. The icy wind stung his face and he pulled his woolen cap lower. It was freezing, but he was in no special hurry to meet this sad man on the eve of Christmas.

Finally, he turned onto Oak and pulled up in the driveway of the small brick house with a steep high roof. The trim of the house was green and the brick was dark red and it was set near the front of an immaculate yard and hedges, carefully manicured, Billy supposed, by someone with a lot of time on his hands.

The man who answered was wearing a heavy sweater and baggy wool trousers. When he reached through the door to take the package, Billy saw him fumble for a minute, then drop a metal object into his pocket, as if to hide it. Still, Billy recognized instantly that the old man had been holding a trumpet mouthpiece in his hand. The thought of it flashed into his mind like an incongruous piece of a puzzle. He was intrigued by the mystery of it. While the old man counted out the change, the delivery boy looked at him and tried to think of the words that might unlock part of the mystery. He wanted to say something. Anything. But what? Then it was too late. He watched the old man take a wrinkled five dollar bill from his pocket, fold it once, and put it in his hand. "This is for you," he said, "and Merry Christmas."

. Billy took the long way back. He turned up through the business district, past the square. The stores were closing now and the streets were almost empty. He turned the corner and saw a young couple swinging a little girl between their arms. The child giggled with delight and the couple laughed. Billy rode past the square another block and turned east toward home.

* * * * *

In the kitchen Brubaker unscrewed the cap and poured another teaspoon of the cough medicine. He put the bottle in the cupboard and glanced again at the clock. Then he turned around, walked slowly into the living room, and took his heavy coat from the closet. Unlatching the back door, he flipped on the porchlight that lighted the little courtyard garden in back, and walked out and sat down on the garden bench.

Brubaker leaned back and closed his eyes, letting his thoughts drift back to Christmases of long ago, Christmases that might have been. He tried to picture the three of them together, laughing, happy. Brubaker sighed heavily and shrugged. In his hands, the silver trumpet reflected in the moonlight. The wind had slowed now and the night was still and quiet. It was almost midnight. Brubaker closed his eyes again. Then he heard it.

It was very faint at first, so soft Brubaker thought he might be dreaming, but then he knew he wasn't. The notes were clear and mellow, ringing like wisps of wind, coming unmistakably from the mountain. With each bar of the Christmas carol, the trumpet's call seemed to grow, like a choir adding voices, like the triumphant march of a musical army. Brubaker felt his emotions welling with each note, till the tears finally flooded his cheeks. Then, like a man in a dream, he picked up the trumpet and, lifting it to his lips, began to play an echo to the mountain serenade, a salute to the unseen musician. Together, the two voices in harmony soared over the notes, calling each to the other's call and showering the silent city with a serenade.

After a long while at the top of the mountain, Billy could still hear the echo pounding in his ears when he reached down and closed the snaps of his trumpet case.

Across town, when the music ended, Sam Smith went over to a window and looked out across his lawn.

"Melinda, come see," he said. "It's snowing."

Health, Peace, and sweet content be yours.
Shakespeare

A Certain Small Shepherd

Rebecca Caudill

This particular story, although only a generation old, is well on its way to becoming a Christmas classic. Once it has been read out loud, most families want it reread again and again, for its message speaks to all of us. It reminds us that we should not ridicule a child and his inward world, for his concept of God's relationship to man may be closer to God's kingdom than is our own.

THIS is a story of a strange and marvelous thing. It happened on a Christmas morning, at Hurricane Gap, and not so long ago at that.

But before you hear about Christmas morning, you must hear about Christmas Eve, for that is part of the story.

And before you hear about Christmas Eve, you must hear about Jamie, for without Jamie there would be no story.

Jamie was born on a freakish night in November. The cold that night moved down from the North and rested its heavy hand suddenly on Hurricane Gap. Within an hour's time the naked earth turned brittle. Line Fork Creek froze solid in its winding bed and lay motionless, like a string dropped at the foot of Pine Mountain.

Nothing but the dark wind was abroad in the hollow. Wild creatures huddled in their dens. Cows stood hunched in their stalls. Housewives stuffed the cracks underneath their doors against the needling cold, and men heaped oak and apple wood on their fires.

At the foot of the gap where Jamie's house stood, the wind doubled its fury. It battered the doors of the house. It rattled the windows. It wailed like a banshee in the chimney. "For sure it's bad luck trying to break in," moaned Jamie's mother, and turned her face to her pillow.

"Bad luck has no business here," Jamie's father said bravely. He laid more logs on the fire. Flames licked at them and roared up the chimney. But through the roaring the wind wailed on, thin and high.

Father took the newborn baby from the bed beside its mother and sat holding it on his knee. "Saro," he called, "you and Honey come and see Jamie!"

Two girls came from the shadows of the room. In the firelight they stood looking at the tiny, wrinkled, red face inside the blanket.

"He's such a little brother!" said Saro.

"Give him time, he'll grow," said Father proudly. "When he's 3, he'll be as big as Honey. When he's 6, he'll be as big as you. You want to hold him?"

Saro sat down on the stool and Father laid the bundle in her arms.

Honey stood beside Saro. She pulled back the corner of the blanket. She opened one of the tiny hands and laid one of her fingers in it. She smiled at the face in the blanket. She looked upward, smiling at Father.

But Father did not see her. He was standing beside Mother, trying to comfort her.

That night Jamie's mother died.

Jamie ate and slept and grew.

Like other babies, he cut teeth. He learned to sit alone, and to crawl. When he was a year old, he toddled about like other 1-year-olds. At 2 he carried around sticks and stones like other 2-year-olds. He threw balls, and built towers of blocks and knocked them down.

Everything that other 2-year-olds could do Jamie could do, except one thing. He could not talk.

The women of Hurricane Gap sat in their chimney corners and shook their heads.

"His mother, poor soul, should have rubbed him with lard," said one.

"She ought to have brushed him with a rabbit's foot," said another.

"Wasn't the boy born on a Wednesday?" asked another. "Wednesday's child is full of woe," she quoted from an old saying.

"Jamie gets everything he wants by pointing," explained Father. "Give him time. He'll learn to talk."

At 3 Jamie could zip his pants and tie his shoes.

At 4 he followed Father to the stable and milked the kittens' pan full of milk. But even at 4 Jamie could not talk like other children. He could only make strange grunting noises.

One day Jamie found a litter of new kittens in a box under the stairs. He ran to the cornfield to tell Father. He wanted to say he had been feeling around in the box for a ball he'd lost, and suddenly his fingers felt something warm and squirmy, and there were all those kittens. But how could you tell somebody something if when you opened your mouth you could only grunt?

Jamie started running. He ran till he reached the orchard. There he threw himself face down in the tall grass and kicked his feet against the ground.

One day Honey's friend came to play hide-and-seek. Jamie played with them. Because Clive was the oldest, he shut his eyes first and counted to 50 while the other children scattered and hid behind trees in the yard and corners of the house. After he had counted to 50, the hollow rang with cries.

"One, two, three for Millie!"

"One, two, three for Jamie!"

"One, two, three for Honey!"

"One, two, three—I'm home free."

It came Jamie's turn to shut his eyes. He sat on the doorstep, covered his eyes with his hands and began to count.

"Listen to Jamie!" Clive called to the other children. The others listened. They all began to laugh.

Jamie got up from the doorstep. He ran after the children. He fought them with both fists and both feet. Honey helped him.

Then Jamie ran away to the orchard and threw himself down on his face in the tall grass and kicked the ground.

Later, when Father was walking through the orchard, he came across Jamie lying in the grass.

"Jamie," said Father, "there's a new calf in the pasture. I need you to help me bring it to the stable."

Jamie got up from the grass. He wiped his eyes. Out of the orchard and across the pasture he trudged at Father's heels. In a far corner of the pasture they found the cow. Beside her, on wobbly legs, stood the new calf.

Together Father and Jamie drove the cow and the calf to the stable, into an empty stall. Together they brought nubbins from the corncrib to feed the cow. Together they made a bed of clean hay for the calf.

"Jamie," said Father the next morning, "I need you to help plow the corn." Father harnessed the horse and lifted Jamie to the horse's back. Away to the cornfield they went, Father walking in front of the horse, Jamie riding, holding tight to the mane.

While Father plowed, Jamie walked in the furrow behind him. When Father lay on his back in the shade of the persimmon tree to rest, Jamie lay beside him. Father told Jamie the names of the birds flying overhead: the turkey vulture lifting and tilting its uplifted wings against the white clouds, the carrion crow flapping lazily and sailing, and the sharp-shinned hawk gliding to rest in the woodland.

The next day Jamie helped Father set out sweet potatoes. Other days he helped Father trim fence rows and mend fences. Whatever Father did, Jamie helped him.

One day Father drove the car out of the shed and stopped in front of the house. "Jamie!" he called. "Jump in. We're going across Pine Mountain."

"Can I go too?" asked Honey.

"Not today," said Father. "I'm taking Jamie to see a doctor."

The doctor looked at Jamie's throat. He listened to Jamie grunt. He shook his head.

"You might see Dr. Jones," he said.

Father and Jamie got into the car and drove across Big Black Mountain to see Dr. Jones.

"Maybe Jamie could learn to talk," said Dr. Jones. "But he would have to be sent away to a special school. He would have to stay there several months. He might even have to stay two or three years. Or four."

"It is a long time," said Dr. Jones.

"And the pocket is empty," said Father.

So Father and Jamie got into the car and started home. Usually Father talked to Jamie as they drove along. Now they drove all the way, across Big Black and across Pine, without a word.

In August, every year, school opened at Hurricane Gap. On the first morning of school, the year that Jamie was 6, Father handed him a book, a tablet, a pencil and a box of crayons, all shiny and new.

"You're going to school, Jamie," he said. "I'll go with you this morning."

The neighbors watched them walking down the road together, toward the little one-room schoolhouse.

"Poor, foolish Father!" they said, and shook their heads. "Trying to make somebody out of that no-account boy!"

Miss Creech, the teacher, shook her head, too. With so many children, so many classes, so many grades, she hadn't time for a boy that couldn't talk, she told Father.

"What will Jamie do all day long?" she asked.

"He will listen," said Father.

So Jamie took his tablet, his pencil, and his box of crayons, and sat down in an empty seat in the front row.

Every day Jamie listened. He learned the words in the pages of his book. He learned how to count. He liked the reading and counting. But the part of school Jamie liked best was the big piece of paper Miss Creech gave him every day. On it he printed words in squares, like the other children. He wrote numbers.

He drew pictures and colored them with his crayons. He could say things on paper.

One day Miss Creech said Jamie had the best paper in the first grade. She held it up for all the children to see.

On sunny days on the playground the children played ball games and three deep and duck-on-a-rock—games a boy can play without talking. On rainy days they played indoors.

One rainy day the children played a guessing game. Jamie knew the answer that no other child could guess. But he couldn't say the answer. He didn't know how to spell the answer. He could only point to show that he knew the answer.

That evening at home he threw his book into the corner. He slammed the door. He pulled Honey's hair. He twisted the cat's tail. The cat yowled and leaped under the bed.

"Jamie," said Father, "cats have feelings, just like boys."

Every year the people of Hurricane Gap celebrated Christmas in the white-steepled church that stood across the road from Jamie's house. On Christmas Eve the boys and girls gave a Christmas play. People came miles to see it, from the other side of Pine Mountain and from the head of every creek and hollow. Miss Creech directed the play.

Through the late fall, as the leaves fell from the trees and the days grew shorter and the air snapped with cold, Jamie wondered when Miss Creech would talk about the play. Finally, one afternoon in November, Miss Creech announced it was time to begin play practice.

Jamie laid his book inside the desk and listened carefully as Miss Creech assigned the parts of the play.

Miss Creech gave the part of Mary to Joan who lived up Pine Mountain, beyond the rock quarry. She asked Honey to bring her big doll to be the baby. She gave the part of Joseph to Henry, who lived at the head of Little Laurelpatch. She asked Saro to be an angel, Clive the innkeeper. She chose three big boys to be people living in Bethlehem. The rest of the boys and girls would sing carols, she said.

Jamie for a moment listened to the sound of the words he had heard. Yes, Miss Creech expected him to sing carols.

Every day after school the boys and girls went with Miss Creech up the road to the church and practiced the Christmas play.

Every day Jamie stood in the front row of the carolers. The first day he stood quietly. The second day he shoved Milly who was standing next to him. The third day he pulled Honey's hair. The fourth day, when the carolers began singing, Jamie ran to the window, grabbed a ball from the sill, and bounced it across the floor.

"Wait a minute, children," Miss Creech said to the children. She turned to Jamie.

"Jamie," she asked, "how would you like to be a shepherd?"

"He's too little," said one of the big shepherds.

"No, he isn't," said Saro. "If my father was a shepherd, Jamie would help him."

That afternoon Jamie became a small shepherd. He ran home after practice to tell Father. Father couldn't understand what Jamie was telling him, but he knew that Jamie had been changed into somebody important.

One afternoon, at play practice, Miss Creech said to the boys and girls, "Forget you are Joan and Henry and Saro and Clive and Jamie. Remember that you are Mary and Joseph, an angel, an innkeeper, and a shepherd, and that strange things are happening in the hollow where you live."

That night at bedtime, Father took the big Bible off the table. Saro and Honey and Jamie gathered around the fire. Over the room a hush fell as Father read: "And there were in the same country shepherds abiding in the field, keeping watch over their flock by night. And, lo, the angel of the Lord came upon them, and the glory of the Lord shone around about them: and they were sore afraid. And the angel said unto them, Fear not: for, behold, I bring you good tidings of great joy, which shall be to all people. . . . And it came to pass, as the angels were gone away from them into heaven, the shepherds said to one another, Let us now go even unto Bethlehem, and see this thing which is come to pass, which the Lord hath made known unto us. And they came with haste, and found Mary, and Joseph, and the babe lying in a manger."

Christmas drew near. At home in the evenings, when they had finished studying their lessons, the boys and girls of Hurricane Gap made decorations for the Christmas tree that would stand in the church. They glued together strips of bright-colored paper in long chains. They whittled stars and baby lambs and camels out of wild cherry wood. They strung long strings of popcorn.

Jamie strung a string of popcorn. Every night as Father read from the Bible, Jamie added more kernels to his string.

"Jamie, are you trying to make a string long enough to reach to the top of Pine Mountain?" asked Honey one night.

Jamie did not hear her. He was far away on a hillside, tending sheep. And even though he was a small shepherd and could only grunt when he tried to talk, an angel wrapped around with dazzling light was singling him out to tell him a wonderful thing had happened down in the hollow in a cow stall. He fell asleep, stringing his popcorn and listening.

In a corner of the room where the fire burned, Father pulled from under his bed the trundle bed in which Jamie slept. He turned back the covers, picked Jamie up from the floor and laid him gently in the bed.

The next day Father went across Pine Mountain to the store. When he came home, he handed Saro a package. In it was cloth of four colors: green, gold, white, and red.

"Make Jamie a shepherd's coat, like the picture in the Bible," Father said to Saro.

Father went into the woods and found a crooked limb of a tree. He made it into a shepherd's crook for Jamie.

Jamie went to school the next morning carrying his shepherd's crook and his shepherd's coat on his arm. He would wear his coat and carry his crook when the boys and girls practiced the play.

All day Jamie waited patiently to practice the play. All day he sat listening. But who could tell whose voice he heard? It might have been Miss Creech's. It might have been an angel's.

Two days before Christmas, Jamie's father and Clive's father drove in a pickup truck along the Trace Branch road, looking for a Christmas tree. On the mountainside they spotted a juniper growing broad and tall and free. With axes they cut it down. They snaked it down the mountainside and loaded it into the truck.

Father had opened the doors of the church wide to get the tree inside. It reached to the ceiling. Frost-blue berries shone on its feathery green branches. The air around it smelled of spice.

That afternoon the mothers of Hurricane Gap, and Miss Creech, and all the boys and girls gathered at the church to decorate the tree.

In the tip-top of the tree they fastened the biggest star. Among the branches they hung other stars, and baby lambs and the camels whittled out of wild cherry wood. They hung chains from branch to branch. Last of all, they festooned the tree with strings of snowy popcorn.

"Ah!" they said, as they stood back and looked at the tree. "Ah!"

Beside the tree the boys and girls practiced the Christmas play for the last time. When they had finished, they started home. Midway down the aisle they turned and looked again at the tree.

Saro opened the door. "Look!" she called, "Look, everybody! It's snowing!"

Jamie, the next morning, looked out on a world such as he had never seen. Hidden were the roads and the fences, the woodpile and the swing under the oak tree, all buried deep under a lumpy quilt of snow. And before a stinging wind, snowflakes still madly whirled and danced.

Saro and Honey joined Jamie at the window.

"You can't see across Line Fork Creek in this storm," said Saro. "And where is Pine Mountain?"

"Where is the church?" asked Honey. "That's what I'd like to know."

Jamie turned to them with questions in his eyes.

"If it had been snowing hard that night in Bethlehem, Jamie," Honey told him, "the shepherds wouldn't have had their sheep out in the pasture. They would have had them in the stable, keeping them warm, wouldn't they, Father? They wouldn't have heard what the angel said, all shut indoors like that."

"When angels have something to tell a shepherd," said Father, "they can find him in any place, in any sort of weather. If the shepherd is listening, he will hear."

At 11:00 the telephone rang.

"Hello!" said Father.

Saro and Honey and Jamie heard Miss Creech's voice, "I've just got the latest weather report. This storm is going on all day, and into the night. Do you think—"

The telephone started ringing, and once it started to ring it wouldn't stop. Everyone in Hurricane Gap listened. The news they heard was always bad. Drifts 10 feet high were piled up along Trace Branch Road. The boys and girls in Little Laurelpatch couldn't get out. Joseph lived in Little Laurelpatch. The road up to the rock quarry . . . Mary couldn't get down the mountain. And then the telephone went silent, dead in the storm.

Meanwhile, the snow kept up its crazy dance before the wind. It drifted in great white mounds across the roads and in the fence rows.

"Nobody but a foolish man would take to the road on a day like this," said Father.

At dinner Jamie sat at the table staring at his plate.

"Shepherds must eat, Jamie," said Father.

"Honey and I don't feel like eating either, Jamie," said Saro, "but see how Honey is eating!"

Still Jamie stared at his plate.

"Know what?" asked Saro. "Because we're all disappointed, we won't save the Christmas stack cake for tomorrow. We'll have a slice today. As soon as you eat your dinner, Jamie."

Still Jamie stared at his plate. He did not touch his food.

"You think that play was real, don't you, Jamie?" said Honey. "It wasn't real. It was just a play we were giving, like some story we'd made up."

Jamie could hold his sobs no longer. His body heaved as he ran to Father. Father laid an arm about Jamie's shoulders.

"Sometimes, Jamie," he said, "angels say to shepherds, 'Be of good courage.' "

On through the short afternoon the storm raged. Father heaped more wood on the fire. Saro sat in front of the fire reading a book. Honey cracked hickory nuts on the stone hearth. Jamie sat.

"Bring the popper, Jamie, and I'll pop some corn for you," said Father.

Jamie shook his head.

"Want me to read to you?" asked Saro.

Jamie shook his head.

"Why don't you help Honey crack hickory nuts?" asked Father.

Jamie shook his head.

"Jamie still thinks he's a shepherd," said Honey.

After a while Jamie left the fire and stood at the window, watching the wild storm. He squinted his eyes and stared—he motioned to his Father to come and look. Saro and Honey, too, hurried to the window and peered out.

Through the snowdrifts trudged a man, followed by a woman. They were bundled and buttoned from head to foot, and their faces were lowered against the wind and the flying snowflakes.

"Lord have mercy!" said Father as he watched them turn in at the gate.

Around the house the man and woman made their way to the back door. As Father opened the door to them, a gust of snow-laden wind whisked into the kitchen.

"Come in out of the cold," said Father.

The man and the woman stepped inside. They stamped their feet on the kitchen floor and brushed the snow from their clothes. They followed Father into the front room and sat down before the fire in the chairs Father told Saro to bring. Father, too, sat down.

Jamie stood beside Father. Saro and Honey stood behind his chair. The three of them stared at the man and the woman silently.

"Where did you come from?" asked Father.

"The other side of Pine Mountain," said the man.

"Why didn't you stop sooner?" said Father.

"We did stop," the man said. "At three houses. Nobody had room," he said.

Father was silent for a minute. He looked at his own bed and at Jamie's trundle bed underneath it. The man and the woman looked numbly into the fire.

"How far were you going?" asked Father.

"Down Straight Creek," said the man. He jerked his head toward the woman. "To her sister's."

"You'll never get there tonight," Father said.

"Maybe—" said the man. "Maybe there'd be a place in your stable."

"We could lay pallets on the kitchen floor," said Father.

The woman looked at the children. She shook her head. "The stable is better," she said.

"The stable is cold," said Father.

"It will do," said the woman.

When the man and the woman had dried their clothes and warmed themselves, Father led the way to the stable. He carried an armload of quilts and on top of them an old buffalo skin. From his right arm swung a lantern and a milk bucket. "I'll milk while I'm there," he said to Saro. "Get supper ready."

Jamie and Saro and Honey watched from the kitchen window as the three trudged through the snowdrifts to the stable.

It was dark when Father came back to the house.

"How long are the man and woman going to stay?" asked Honey.

Father hung a teakettle of water on the crane over the fire and went upstairs to find another lantern.

"All night tonight," he said as he came down the stairs. "Maybe longer."

Father hurriedly ate the supper Saro put on the table. Then he took in one hand the lighted lantern and a tin bucket filled with supper for the man and the woman.

"I put some Christmas stack cake in the bucket," said Saro.

In his other hand, Father took the teakettle.

"It's cold in that stable," he said, as he started out the kitchen door. "Bitter cold."

On the door step he turned. "Don't wait up for me," he called back. "I may be gone a good while."

Over the earth darkness thickened. Still the wind blew and the snow whirled. The clock on the mantle struck 8:00. It ticked solemnly in the quiet house where Saro and Honey and Jamie waited.

"Why doesn't Father come?" complained Honey.

"Why don't you hang up your stocking and go to bed?" asked Saro. "Jamie, it's time to hang up your stocking, too, and go to bed."

Jamie did not answer. He sat staring into the fire.

"That Jamie! He still thinks he's a shepherd," said Honey as she hung her stocking under the mantle.

"Jamie," said Saro, "aren't you going to hang up your stocking and go to bed?" She pulled the trundle bed from beneath Father's bed and turned back the covers. She turned back the covers on Father's bed.

She hung up her stocking and followed Honey upstairs.

"Jamie!" she called out.

Still Jamie stared into the fire. A strange feeling was growing inside him. This night was not like other nights, he knew. Something mysterious was going on. He felt afraid.

What was that he heard? The wind? Only the wind?

He lay down on the bed with his clothes on. He dropped off to sleep. A rattling at the door wakened him.

He sat upright quickly. He looked around. His heart beat fast. But nothing in the room had changed. Everything was as it had been when he lay down. The fire was burning, two stockings, Saro's and Honey's, hung under the mantle, the clock was ticking solemnly.

He looked at Father's bed. The sheets were just as Saro had turned them back.

There! There it was again! It sounded like singing. "Glory to God! On earth peace!"

Jamie breathed hard. Had he heard that? Or had he only said it to himself? He lay down again and pulled the quilts over his head.

"Get up, Jamie," he heard Father saying. "Put your clothes on quick."

Jamie opened his eyes. He saw daylight filling the room. He saw Father standing over him, bundled in warm clothes.

Wondering, Jamie flung the quilts back and rolled out of bed.

"Why, Jamie," said Father, "you're already dressed!"

Father went to the stairs. "Saro! Honey!" he called. "Come quick!"

"What's happened, Father?" asked Saro.

"What are we going to do?" asked Honey as she fumbled sleepily with her shoelaces.

"Come with me," said Father.

"Where are we going?" asked Honey.

"To the stable?" asked Saro.

"The stable was no fit place," said Father. "Not when the church was close by, and it with a stove in it, and coal for burning."

Out into the cold, silent, white morning they went. The wind had died. The clouds were lifting. One star in the vast sky, its brilliance fading in the growing light, shone down on Hurricane Gap.

Father led the way through the drifted snow. The others followed, stepping in his tracks. As Father pushed open the church door, the fragrance of the Christmas tree rushed out at them. The potbellied stove glowed red with the fire within.

Muffling his footsteps, Father walked quietly up the aisle. Wonderingly, the others followed. There, beside the star-crowned Christmas tree where the Christmas play was to have been given, they saw the woman. She lay on the old buffalo skin, covered with quilts. Beside her pallet sat the man.

The woman smiled at them. "You came to see?"

41

she asked, and lifted the cover.

Saro went first and peeped under the cover. Honey went next.

"You look, too, Jamie," said Saro.

For a moment Jamie hesitated. He leaned forward and took one quick look. Then he turned, shot down the aisle and out of the church, slamming the door behind him.

Saro ran down the church aisle, calling after him.

"Wait, Saro," said Father, watching Jamie through the window.

To the house Jamie made his way, half running along the path Father's big boots had cut through the snowdrifts.

Inside the house he hurriedly pulled his shepherd's robe over his coat. He snatched up his crook from the chimney corner.

With his hand on the doorknob, he glanced toward the fireplace. There, under the mantel, hung Saro's and Honey's stockings. And there, beside them, hung his stocking! Now who had hung it there? It had in it the same bulge his stocking had had every Christmas morning since he could remember, a bulge made by an orange.

Jamie ran to the fireplace and felt the toe of his stocking. Yes, there was the dime, just as on other Christmas mornings.

Hurriedly he emptied his stocking. With the orange and the dime in one hand and the crook in the other, he made his way toward the church. Father and Saro, still watching, saw his shepherd's robe—a spot of glowing color in a great white world.

Father opened the church door.

Without looking to the left or right, Jamie hurried up the aisle. Father and Saro followed him. Beside the pallet he dropped to his knees.

"Here is a Christmas gift for the child," he said, clear and strong.

"Father!" gasped Saro. "Father, listen to Jamie!"

The woman turned back the covers from the baby's face. Jamie gently laid the orange beside the baby's tiny hand.

"And here's a gift for the mother," Jamie said to the woman. He put the dime in her hand.

"Surely," the woman spoke softly, "the Lord lives this day."

"Surely," said Father, "the Lord does live this day, and all days. And He is loving and merciful and good."

In the hush that followed, Christmas in all its joys and its majesty came to Hurricane Gap. And it wasn't so long ago at that.

A String of Blue Beads

Fulton Oursler

One of the loveliest of all Christmas short stories was penned by Fulton Oursler. Oursler's story reminds us that possessions without someone to share them with are hollow and meaningless. He also reminds us once again that one can't pay more than "all one has" for a gift.

PETE Richards was the loneliest man in town on the day Jean Grace opened his door. You may have seen something in the newspapers about the incident at the time it happened, although neither his name nor hers was published, nor was the full story told as I tell it here.

Pete's shop had come down to him from his grandfather. The little front window was strewn with a disarray of old-fashioned things: bracelets and lockets worn in days before the Civil War, gold rings and silver boxes, images of jade and ivory, porcelain figurines.

On this winter's afternoon a child was standing there, her forehead against the glass, earnest and enormous eyes studying each discarded treasure as if she were looking for something quite special. Finally she straightened up with a satisfied air and entered the store.

The shadowy interior of Pete Richards' establishment was even more cluttered than his show window. Shelves were stacked with jewel caskets, dueling pistols, clocks, and lamps, and the floor was heaped with andirons and mandolins and things hard to find a name for.

Behind the counter stood Pete himself, a man not more than 30 but with hair already turning gray. There was a bleak air about him as he looked at the small customer who flattened her ungloved hands on the counter.

"Mister," she began, "would you please let me look at that string of blue beads in the window?"

Pete parted the draperies and lifted out a necklace. The turquoise stones gleamed brightly against the pallor of his palm as he spread the ornament before her.

"They're just perfect," said the child, entirely to herself. "Will you wrap them up pretty for me, please?"

Pete studied her with a stony air. "Are you buying these for someone?"

"They're for my big sister. She takes care of me.

43

You see, this will be the first Christmas since Mother died. I've been looking for the most wonderful Christmas present for my sister."

"How much money do you have?" asked Pete warily.

She had been busily untying the knots in a handkerchief and now she poured out a handful of pennies on the counter.

"I emptied my bank," she explained simply.

Pete Richards looked at her thoughtfully. Then he carefully drew back the necklace. The price tag was visible to him but not to her. How could he tell her? The trusting look of her blue eyes smote him like the pain of an old wound.

"Just a minute," he said, and turned toward the back of the store. Over his shoulder he called, "What's your name?" He was very busy about something.

"Jean Grace."

When Pete returned to where Jean Grace waited, a package lay in his hand, wrapped in scarlet paper and tied with a bow of green ribbon. "There you are," he said shortly. "Don't lose it on the way home."

She smiled happily at him over her shoulder as she ran out the door. Through the window he watched her go, while desolation flooded his thoughts. Something about Jean Grace and her string of beads had stirred him to the depths of a grief that would not stay buried. The child's hair was wheat yellow, her eyes sea blue, and once upon a time, not long before, Pete had been in love with a girl with hair of that same

yellow and with eyes just as blue. And the turquoise necklace was to have been hers.

But there had come a rainy night—a truck skidding on a slippery road—and the life was crushed out of his dream.

Since then Pete Richards had lived too much with his grief in solitude. He was politely attentive to customers, but after business hours his world seemed irrevocably empty. He was trying to forget in a self-pitying haze that deepened day by day.

The blue eyes of Jean Grace jolted him into acute remembrance of what he had lost. The pain of it made him recoil from the exuberance of holiday shoppers. During the next 10 days trade was brisk; chattering women swarmed in, fingering trinkets, trying to bargain. When the last customer had gone, late on Christmas Eve, he sighed with relief. It was over for another year. But for Pete Richards the night was not quite over.

The door opened and a young woman hurried in. With an inexplicable start, he realized that she looked familiar, yet he could not remember when or where he had seen her before. Her hair was golden yellow and her large eyes were blue. Without speaking, she drew from her purse a package loosely unwrapped in its red paper, a bow of green ribbon with it. Presently the string of blue beads lay gleaming again before him.

"Did this come from your shop?" she asked.

Pete raised his eyes to hers and answered softly, "Yes, it did."

"Are the stones real?"

"Yes. Not the finest quality—but real."

"Can you remember who it was you sold them to?"

"She was a small girl. Her name was Jean. She bought them for her older sister's Christmas present."

"How much are they worth?"

"The price," he told her solemnly, "is always a confidential matter between the seller and the customer."

"But Jean has never had more than a few pennies of spending money. How could she pay for them?"

Pete was folding the gay paper back into its creases, rewrapping the little package just as neatly as before.

"She paid the biggest price anyone can ever pay," he said. "She gave all she had."

There was a silence then that filled the little curio shop. He saw the faraway steeple, a bell began ringing. The sound of the distant chiming, the little package lying on the counter, the question in the eyes of the girl, and the strange feeling of renewal struggling unreasonably in the heart of the man, all had come to be because of the love of a child.

"But why did you do it?"

He held out the gift in his hand.

"It's already Christmas morning," he said. "And it's my misfortune that I have no one to give anything to. Will you let me see you home and wish you a Merry Christmas at your door?"

And so, to the sound of many bells and in the midst of happy people, Pete Richards and a girl whose name he had yet to hear, walked out into the beginning of the great day that brings hope into the world for us all.

David's Star of Bethlehem

Christine Whiting Parmenter

I was still young when I first remember my mother reciting this particular story. It's a story I defy any red-blooded human to listen to—or read—dry-eyed. All the tragedy of cruelty, loss, inhumanity, and death are here, just as are the sublimity of love, caring, restoration, and happiness. Through the years it has become a Christmas season classic.

SCOTT Carson reached home in a bad humor. Nancy, slipping a telltale bit of red ribbon into her work-basket, realized this as soon as he came in.

It was the twenty-first of December, and a white Christmas was promised. Snow had been falling for hours, and in most of the houses wreaths were already in the windows. It was what one calls "a Christmasy-feeling day," yet, save for that red ribbon in Nancy's basket, there was no sign in the Carson home of the approaching festival.

Scott said, kissing her absent-mindedly and slumping into a big chair, "This snow is the very limit. If the wind starts blowing there'll be a fierce time with the traffic. My train was 20 minutes late as it was, and—there's the bell. Who can it be at this hour? I want my dinner."

"I'll go to the door," said Nancy hurriedly, as he started up. "Selma's putting dinner on the table now."

Relaxing into his chair, Scott heard her open the front door, say something about the storm and, after a moment, wish someone a Merry Christmas.

A Merry Christmas! He wondered that she could say it so calmly. Three years ago on Christmas morning, they had lost their boy—swiftly—terribly—without warning. Meningitis, the doctor said. Only a few hours before, the child had seemed a healthy, happy youngster, helping them trim the tree; hoping, with a twinkle in the brown eyes so like his mother's, that Santa Claus would remember the fact that he wanted skis! He had gone happily to bed after Nancy had read them "The Night Before Christmas," a custom of early childhood's days that the 11-year-old lad still clung to. Later his mother remembered, with a pang, that when she kissed him good night he had said his head felt "kind of funny." But she had left him light-heartedly enough and gone down to help Scott fill the stockings. Santa had not forgotten the skis;

but Jimmy never saw them.

Three years—and the memory still hurt so much that the very thought of Christmas was agony to Scott Carson. Jimmy had slipped away just as the carolers stopped innocently beneath his window, their voices rising clear and penetrating on the dawn-sweet air:

"Silent night, holy night . . ."

Scott rose suddenly. He *must* not live over that time again. "Who was it?" he asked gruffly as Nancy joined him, and understanding the gruffness she answered tactfully, "Only the expressman."

"What'd he bring?"

"Just a—a package."

"One naturally supposes that," replied her husband, with a touch of sarcasm. Then, suspicion gripping him, he burst out, "Look here! If you've been getting a Christmas gift for me, I—I won't have it. I told you I wanted to forget Christmas. I—"

"I know, dear," she broke in hastily. "The package was only from Aunt Mary."

"Didn't you tell her we weren't keeping Christmas?" he demanded, irritably.

"Yes, Scott; but—but you know Aunt Mary! Come now, dinner's on and I think it's a good one. You'll feel better after you eat."

But Scott found it unaccountably hard to eat; and later, when Nancy was reading aloud in an effort to soothe him, he could not follow. She had chosen something humorous and diverting; but in the midst of a paragraph he spoke, and she knew that he had not been listening.

"Nancy," he said, "is there anyplace—anyplace on God's earth where we can get away from Christmas?"

She looked up, answering with sweet gentleness, "It would be a hard place to find, Scott."

He faced her suddenly. "I feel as if I couldn't stand it—the trees—the carols—the merrymaking, you know. Oh, if I could only sleep this week away! But . . . I've been thinking . . . Would—would you consider for one moment going up to camp with me for a day or two? I'd go alone, but—"

"Alone!" she echoed. "Up there in the wilderness at Christmas time? Do you think I'd let you?"

"But it would be hard for you, dear, cold and uncomfortable. I'm a brute to ask it, and yet—"

Nancy was thinking rapidly. They could not escape Christmas, of course. No change of locality could make them forget the anniversary of the day that Jimmy went away. But she was worried about Scott, and the change of scene might help him over the difficult hours ahead. The camp, situated on the mountain a mile from any neighbors, would at least be isolated. There was plenty of bedding, and a big fireplace. It was worth trying.

She said, cheerfully, "I'll go with you, dear. Perhaps the change will make things easier for both of us."

This was Tuesday, and on Thursday afternoon they stepped off the north-bound train and stood on the platform watching it vanish into the mountains. The day was crisp and cold! "Two above," the stationmaster told them as they went into the box of a station and moved instinctively toward the red-hot "air-tight" stove which gave forth grateful warmth.

"I sent a telegram yesterday to Clem Hawkins, over on the mountain road," said Scott. "I know you don't deliver a message so far off; but I took a chance. Do you know if he got it?"

"Yep. Clem don't have a 'phone, but the boy came down for some groceries and I sent it up. If I was you, though, I'd stay to the Central House. Seems as if it would be more cheerful—Christmas time."

"I guess we'll be comfortable enough if Hawkins airs out, and lights a fire," replied Scott, his face hardening at this innocent mention of the holiday. "Is there anyone around here who'll take us up? I'll pay well for it, of course."

"Ira Morse'll go; but you'll have to walk from Hawkinses. The road ain't dug out beyond . . . There's Ira now. You wait, an' I'll holler to him. Hey, Ira!" he called, going to the door. "Will you carry these folks up to Hawkinses? They'll pay for it."

"Iry," a ruddy-faced young farmer, obligingly appeared, his gray workhorse hitched to a one-seated sleigh of ancient and uncomfortable design.

"Have to sit three on a seat," he explained cheerfully, "but we'll be all the warmer for it. Tuck the buffalo robe 'round the lady's feet, mister, and you and me'll use the horse blanket. Want to stop to the store for provisions?"

"Yes, I brought some canned stuff, but we'll need other things," said Nancy. "I've made a list."

"Well, you got good courage," grinned the stationmaster. "I hope you don't get froze to death up in the woods. Merry Christmas to you, anyhow."

"The same to you!" responded Nancy, smiling, and noted with a stab of pain that her husband's sensitive lips were trembling.

Under Ira's cheerful conversation, however, Scott relaxed. They talked of crops, the neighbors, and local politics—safe subjects all; but as they passed the district school, where a half dozen sleighs or flivers were parked, the man explained: "Folks decoratin' the school for the doin's tomorrow afternoon. Christmas tree for the kids, and pieces spoke, and singin'. We got a real live schoolma'am this year, believe me!"

They had reached the road that wound up the mountain toward the Hawkins farm, and as they plodded on, a sudden wind arose that cut their faces. Snow creaked under the runners, and as the sun sank behind the mountain Nancy shivered, not so much with cold as with a sense of loneliness and isolation. It was Scott's voice that roused her:

"Should have brought snowshoes. I didn't realize that we couldn't be carried all the way."

"Guess you'll get there all right," said Ira. "Snow's packed hard as a drumhead, and it ain't likely to thaw yet a while. Here you are," as he drew up before the weather-beaten, unpainted farmhouse. "You better step inside a minute and warm up."

48

A shrewish-looking woman was already at the door, opening it but a crack, in order to keep out fresh air and cold.

"I think," said Nancy, with a glance at the deepening shadows, "that we'd better keep right on. I wonder if there's anybody here who'd help carry our bags and provisions."

"There ain't," answered the woman, stepping outside and pulling a faded gray sweater around her shoulders. "Clem's gone to East Conroy with the eggs, and Dave's up to the camp keepin' yer fire going! You can take the sled and carry yer stuff on that. There 'tis, by the gate. Dave'll bring it back when he comes. An' tell him to hurry. Like as not, Clem won't be back in time fer milkin'."

"I thought Dave was goin' to help Teacher decorate the school this afternoon," ventured Ira. He was unloading their things as he spoke, and roping them to the sled.

"So'd he," responded the woman. "But there w'ant no one else to light that fire, was they? Guess it won't hurt him none to work for his livin' like other folks. That new schoolma'am, she thinks o' nothin' but—"

"Oh, look here!" said the young man, straightening up, a belligerent light in his blue eyes, "it's Christmas! Can Dave go back with me if I stop and milk for him? They'll be workin' all evenin'—lots o' fun for a kid like him, and—"

"No, he can't!" snapped the woman. "His head's enough turned now with speakin' pieces and singin' silly songs. You better be gettin' on, folks. I can't stand here talkin' til mornin'."

She slammed the door, while Ira glared after her retreating figure, kicked the gate post to relieve his feelings, and then grinned sheepishly.

"Some grouch! Why, she didn't even ask you in to get warm! Well, I wouldn't loiter if I was you. And send that kid right back, or he'll get worse'n a tongue-lashin'. Well, goodbye to you, folks. Hope you have a Merry Christmas."

The tramp up the mountain passed almost entirely in silence, for it took their united energy to drag the sled up that steep grade against the wind. Scott drew a breath of relief when they beheld the camp, a spiral of smoke rising from its big stone chimney like a welcome promise of warmth.

"Looks good, doesn't it? But it'll be dark before that boy gets home. I wonder how old—"

They stopped simultaneously as a clear, sweet voice sounded from within the cabin:

"Silent night, holy night . . ."

Scott's face went suddenly dead white. He threw out a hand as if to brush something away, but Nancy caught it in hers, pulling it close against her wildly beating heart.

"All is calm . . . all is bright."

The childish treble came weirdly from within, while Nancy cried, "Scott—dearest, don't let go! It's only the little boy singing the carols he's learned in school. Don't you see? Come! Pull yourself together. We must go in."

Even as she spoke the door swung open, and through blurred vision they beheld the figure of a boy standing on the threshold. He was a slim little boy with an old, oddly wistful face, and big brown eyes under a thatch of yellow hair.

"You the city folks that was comin' up? Here, I'll help carry in your things."

Before either could protest he was down on his knees in the snow, untying Ira's knots with skillful fingers. He would have lifted the heavy suitcase himself had not Scott, jerked back to the present by the boy's action, interfered.

"I'll carry that in." His voice sounded queer and shaky. "You take the basket. We're late, I'm afraid. You'd better hurry home before it gets too dark. Your mother said—"

"I don't mind the dark," said the boy quietly, as they went within. "I'll coast most o' the way down, anyhow. Guess you heard me singin' when you come along." He smiled a shy, embarrassed smile as he explained: "It was a good chance to practice the Christmas carols. They won't let me, 'round home. We're goin' to have a show at the school tomorrow. I'm one o' the three kings—you know—'We Three Kings of Orient Are.' I sing the first verse all by myself," he added with childish pride.

There followed a moment's silence. Nancy was fighting a desire to put her arms about the slim boyish figure, while Scott had turned away, unbuckling the straps of his suitcase with fumbling hands.

Then Nancy said, "I'm afraid we've kept you from helping at the school this afternoon. I'm so sorry."

The boy drew a resigned breath that struck her as strangely unchildlike.

"You needn't mind, ma'am. Maybe they wouldn't have let me go anyway; and I've got tomorrow to think about. I—I been reading one o' your books. I like to read."

"What book was it? Would you like to take it home with you for a—" she glanced at Scott, still on his knees by the suitcase, and finished hurriedly—"a Christmas gift?"

"Wouldn't I?" His wistful eyes brightened, then clouded. "Is there a place maybe where I could hide it 'round here? They don't like me to read much to home. They"—a hard look crept into his young eyes— "they burned up a book Teacher gave me a while back. It was *David Copperfield*, and I hadn't got it finished."

There came a crash as Scott, rising suddenly, upset a chair. The child jumped, and then laughed at himself for being startled.

"Look here, sonny," said Scott huskily, "you must be getting home. Can you bring us some milk tomorrow? I'll find a place to hide your book and tell you about it then. Haven't you got a warmer coat than this?"

He lifted a shabby jacket from the settee and held it out while the boy slipped into it.

"Thanks, mister," he said. "It's hard gettin' it on because it's tore inside. They's only one button," he added, as Scott groped for them. "She don't get much time to sew 'em on. I'll bring up the milk tomorrow mornin'. I got to hurry now or I'll get fits! Thanks for the book, ma'am. I'd like *it* better'n anything. Good night."

Standing at the window, Nancy watched him start out in the fast-descending dusk. It hurt her to think of the lonely walk, but she thrust the thought aside and turned to Scott, who had lighted a fire on the hearth and seemed absorbed in the dancing flames.

"That's good!" she said cheerfully. "I'll get things started for supper, and then make the bed. I'm weary enough to turn in early. You might bring me the canned stuff in your suitcase, Scott. A hot soup ought to taste good tonight."

She took an apron from her bag and moved toward the tiny kitchen. Dave evidently knew how to build a fire. The stove lids were almost red, and the kettle was singing. Nancy went about her preparations deftly, tired though she was from the unaccustomed tramp, while Scott opened a can of soup, toasted some bread, and carried their meal on a tray to the settles before the hearthfire. It was all very cozy and "Christmasy," thought Nancy, with the wind blustering outside and the flames leaping up the chimney. But she was strangely quiet. The thought of that lonely little figure trudging off in the gray dusk persisted, despite her efforts to forget. It was Scott who spoke, saying out of a silence, "I wonder how old he is."

"The—the little boy?"

He nodded, and she answered gently, "He seemed no older than—I mean he seemed very young to be milking cows and doing chores."

Again Scott nodded, and a moment passed before he said, "The work wouldn't hurt him, though, if he were strong enough; but—did you notice, Nancy, he didn't look half fed? He is an intelligent little chap, though, and his voice— Goodness!" he broke off suddenly, "how can a shrew like that bring such a child into the world? To burn his book! Nancy, I can't understand how things are ordered. Here's that poor boy struggling for development in an unhappy atmosphere—and our Jimmy, who had love, and understanding, and— Tell me, why is it?"

She stretched out a tender hand; but the question remained unanswered, and the meal was finished in silence.

Dave did not come with the milk next morning. They waited till nearly noon, and then tramped off in the snow-clad, pine-scented woods. It was a glorious day, with diamonds sparkling on every fir tree, and they came back refreshed and ravenous for their delayed meal. Scott wiped the dishes, whistling as he worked. It struck his wife that he hadn't whistled like that for months. Later, the last kitchen rites accomplished, she went to the window, where he stood gazing down the trail.

"He won't come now, Scott."

"The kid? It's not 3:00 yet, Nancy."

"But the party begins at 4:00. I suppose everyone for miles around will be there. I wish—" She was about to add that she wished they could have gone too, but something in Scott's face stopped the words. She said instead, "Do you think we'd better go for the milk ourselves?"

"What's the use? They'll all be at the shindig, even that sour-faced woman, I suppose. But somehow—I feel worried about the boy. If he isn't here bright and early in the morning, I'll go down and see what's happened. Looks as if it were clouding up again, doesn't it? Perhaps we'll get snowed in!"

Big, lazy-looking snowflakes were already beginning to drift down. Scott piled more wood on the fire, and stretched out on the settee for a nap. But Nancy was restless. She found herself standing repeatedly at the window, looking at the snow. She was there when at last Scott stirred and wakened. He sat up blinking, and asked, noting the twilight, "How long have I been asleep?"

Nancy laughed, relieved to hear his voice after the long stillness.

"It's after 5:00."

"Good thunder!" He arose, putting an arm across her shoulders. "Poor girl! I haven't been much company on this trip! But I didn't sleep well last night, couldn't get that boy out of my mind. Why, look!" Scott was staring out the window into the growing dusk. "Here he is now. I thought you said—"

He was already at the door, flinging it wide in welcome as he went out to lift the box of milk jars

from the sled. It seemed to Nancy, as the child stepped inside, that he looked subtly different—discouraged, she would have said of an older person; and when he raised his eyes she saw the unmistakable sign of recent tears.

"Oh, David!" she exclaimed. "Why aren't you at the party?"

"I didn't go."

The boy seemed curiously to have withdrawn into himself. His answer was like a gentle "none of your business," but Nancy was not without knowledge of boy nature. She thought, *He's hurt—dreadfully. He's afraid to talk for fear he'll cry; but he'll feel better to get it off his mind.* She said, drawing him toward the cheerful hearthfire, "But why not, Dave?"

He swallowed, pulling himself together with a heroic effort.

"I had ter milk. The folks have gone to Conroy to Gramma Hawkins's! I *like* Gramma Hawkins. She told 'em to be sure an' bring me; but there wasn't no one else ter milk, so . . . so . . ."

It was Scott who came to the rescue as David's voice failed suddenly.

"Are you telling us that your people have gone away, for *Christmas*, leaving you home alone?"

The boy nodded, winking back tears as he managed a pathetic smile.

"Oh, I wouldn't ha' minded so much if—if it hadn't been for the doin's at the school. Miss Mary was countin' on me ter sing, and speak a piece. I don't know who they could ha' got to be that wise man."

His face hardened in a way not good to see in a little boy, and he burst out angrily, "Oh, I'd have gone—after they got off! But they hung 'round till almost 4:00, and—when I went for my good suit they—they'd *hid* it—or carried it away! . . . And there was a Christmas tree . . ."

His voice faltered again, while Nancy found herself speechless before what she recognized as a devastating disappointment. She glanced at Scott, coming forward calmly, laying a steady hand on the boy's shoulder. He said—and, knowing what the words cost him, Nancy's heart went out to her husband in adoring gratitude—"Buck up, old scout! We'll have a Christmas tree! And we'll have a party too, you and Mother and I. You can speak your piece and sing your carols for us. And Mother will read us 'The' "—for an appreciable moment Scott's voice faltered, but he went on gamely—" 'The Night Before Christmas.' Did you ever hear it? And I know some stunts that'll make your eyes shine. We'll have our party tomorrow, Christmas Day, sonny; but now" (he was stooping for his overshoes as he spoke), "now we'll go after the tree before it gets too dark! Come on, Mother. We want you, too!"

Mother! Scott hadn't called her that since Jimmy left them! Through tear-blinded eyes Nancy groped for her coat in the diminutive closet. Darkness was coming swiftly as they went into the snowy forest, but they found their tree, and stopped to cut fragrant green branches for decoration. Not till the tree stood proudly in the corner did they remember the lack of tinsel trimmings; but Scott brushed this aside as a mere nothing.

"We've got popcorn, and nothing's prettier. Give us a bit of supper, Nancy, and then I'm going to the village."

"The village! At this hour?"

"You take my sled, mister," cried David, and they saw that his eyes were happy once more, and childlike. "You can coast 'most all the way, like lightning! I'll pop the corn. I'd love to! Boy! It's lucky I milked before I came away!"

The hours that followed passed like magic to Nancy Carson. Veritable wonders were wrought in that small cabin; and oh, it was good to be planning and playing again with a little boy! Not till the child, who had been up since dawn, had dropped asleep on the settee from sheer weariness did she add the finishing touches to the scene.

"It's like a picture of Christmas," she murmured happily. "The tree, so green and slender with its own trimmings, the cone-laden pine at the windows, the bulging stocking at the fireplace, and—and the sleeping boy. I wonder—"

She turned, startled by a step on the creaking snow outside, but it was Scott, of course. He came in silently, not laden with bundles as she'd expected, but empty-handed. There was, she thought, a strange excitement in his manner as he glanced 'round the fire-lit room, his eyes resting for a moment on David's peaceful face. Then he saw the well-filled stocking at the mantel, and his eyes came back unswerving to hers.

"Nancy! Is—is it—?"

She drew nearer, and put her arms around him.

"Yes, dear, it's—Jimmy's—just as we filled it on Christmas Eve three years ago. You see, I couldn't quite bear to leave it behind us when we came away, lying there in his drawer so lonely—at Christmas time. Tell me you don't mind, Scott—won't you? We have our memories, but David—he has so little. That dreadful mother, and—"

Scott cleared his throat, swallowed, and said gently, "He has, I think, the loveliest mother in the world!"

"What do you mean?"

He drew her down onto the settee that faced the sleeping boy and answered, "Listen, Nancy, I went to the schoolhouse. I thought perhaps they'd give me something to trim the tree. The party was over, but the teacher was there with Ira Morse, clearing things away. I told them about David—why he hadn't shown up; and asked some questions. Nancy—what do you think? That Hawkins woman isn't the child's mother! I *knew* it.

"Nobody around here ever saw her. She died when David was a baby, and his father, half-crazed, the natives thought, with grief, brought the child here, and lived like a hermit on the mountain. He died when Dave was about 6, and as no one claimed the youngster, and there was no orphan asylum within miles, he was sent to the poor farm, and stayed there until last year, when Clem Hawkins wanted a boy to help do chores, and Dave was the cheapest thing in sight. Guess you wonder where I've been all this time? Well, I've been interviewing the overseer of the poor—destroying red tape by the yard—resorting to bribery and corruption! But— Hello, did I wake you up?"

David roused suddenly, rubbed his eyes. Then, spying the stocking, he wakened thoroughly and asked, "Say! Is—is this Christmas?"

Scott laughed, and glanced at his watch.

"It will be, in 12 minutes. Come here, sonny."

He drew the boy onto his knee and went on quietly: "The stores were closed, David, when I reached the village. I couldn't buy you a Christmas gift, you see. But I thought if we gave you a *real mother* and—and—a *father*—"

"Oh, Scott!"

It was a cry of rapture from Nancy. She had, of course, suspected the ending to his story, but not until that moment had she let herself really believe it. Then, seeing the child's bewilderment, she explained, "He means, dear, that you're our boy now—for always."

David looked up, his brown eyes bugged out with wonder.

"And I needn't go back to Hawkins's? Not *ever*?"

"Not ever," Scott promised, while his throat tightened at the relief in the boy's voice.

"And I'll have folks, same as the other kids?"

"You've guessed right." The new father spoke lightly in an effort to conceal his feeling. "That is, if you think we'll do!" he added, smiling.

"Oh, you'll—"

Suddenly inarticulate, David turned, throwing his thin arms around Scott's neck in a strangling, boylike hug. Then, a bit ashamed because such things were new to him, he slipped away, standing with his back to them at the window, trying, they saw with understanding hearts, to visualize this unbelievable thing that had come—a miracle—into his starved life. When, after a silence, they joined him, the candle on the table flared up for a protesting moment and then went out. Only starlight and firelight lit the cabin now; and Nancy, peering into the night, said gently, "How beautifully it has cleared. I think I never saw the stars so bright."

"Christmas stars," Scott reminded her and, knowing the memory that brought the roughness to his voice, she caught and clasped his hand..

It was David who spoke next. He was leaning close to the window, his elbows resting on the sill, his face cupped in his two hands. He seemed to have forgotten them as he said dreamily, "It's Christmas . . . Silent night . . . holy night . . . like the song. I wonder"—he looked up trustfully into the faces above him—"I wonder if—if maybe one of them stars isn't the Star of Bethlehem!"

The Red Mittens

Hartley F. Dailey

Oh, how often we judge a person by the mask, just as we do a house by its facade—and fail to see the treasure inside! There is no better master key than kindness.

By the way, it is one of this year's serendipities that, in tracking down permission to use this story, Hartley Dailey himself—still living in a small Ohio town—came into my life, becoming a cherished friend.

I THINK I really count my Christmases from the year Linda was 8. That is the year when "Peace on earth, good will to men" first began to mean something to me.

That was in '34, the worst year of the Great Depression, at least for farmers. Like many another, I had bought a quarter section, 160 acres, just before the market crash, and at much too high a price. Now, with farm prices at rock bottom, the prices of things we had to buy were rising. It took every cent we could scrape together just to pay the interest on the place.

That was the year we decided we just couldn't afford to buy Christmas presents. For ourselves—Jane and I—we didn't mind, but for Linda, we felt differently. Our only child, she seemed almost a baby. She was a serious-minded little girl, with a wealth of silky brown hair and a pair of enormous brown eyes, so warm they would have melted the heart of the legendary "Snow Queen." We felt she was just too young to understand why there was no money to buy presents.

There was a beautiful light-blue coat, just Linda's size, in the window of Lloyd's department store, in the county seat. Every time we'd go to town she'd go and stare into that store window to see if it was still there. But the price was an impossible $12.95! It might just as well have been $100. Jane went to great pains remaking a coat of her own, to fit Linda, and she wore it dutifully. But it could not take the place of the one in Lloyd's window.

In those days our nearest neighbor was Old Man Riggs, whose 500 acres lay between our place and the river. Old Charley Riggs was the stingiest man in three counties, with a disposition like a sour apple and an expression on his face that hinted his chief diet was unripe persimmons. He was reputed to have money, but you never would have guessed it. He dressed like a tramp, and he drove a broken-down old Model T. He never put side-curtains on it, no matter how cold the weather. He'd sit bolt upright, his big, knobby hands holding the steering wheel in a grip like death. I never saw him wear a pair of gloves—not until after that Christmas.

One of the most pressing problems for a farmer in the hill country is water. If you don't have access to a spring or a stream, you must have deep wells to get it. And at that time, before electricity came to the hills, you pumped it by hand. And pumping all the water for all the animals on a farm is labor, indeed.

I had been trying for years to negotiate a right-of-way across Old Man Riggs' place, to the river. Here I was, spending half my time pumping water, while across the narrowest point in Riggs' place, 50 yards from my pasture, was a whole river full! And it wasn't as if he needed it. He had over a mile of frontage— and he wouldn't sell me an inch!

As Christmas approached, Jane was busy going through the attic, picking out things to make, or remake, and for materials to decorate with. Linda was an interested spectator. Then, one day, she came to me with a suggestion. "I want to give Mr. Riggs a Christmas present!" she said.

I was thunderstruck! But I said, "What could you give Mr. Riggs, Linda?"

"I'd have Mother make him some mittens, like she makes for you," came Linda's confident answer.

"Why," I blurted, "the old man would be too stingy to wear them, if you did."

I saw at once that I had made a mistake, for Linda hung her pretty head, and began making circles with her toe, in a way she had. "Mr Riggs is my friend," she said. "He lets me eat pears from that big tree in his yard."

I wouldn't have been more surprised if she had said she had trained one of the local wild cats to catch mice in the kitchen. But, knowing her as I did, I shouldn't have been surprised, even at that. Myself, I wouldn't have given the old tightwad the time of day from his own watch, but I couldn't deny Linda anything, when she looked like that. Besides, I saw the hand of Jane in this, for Jane, the gentlest and sweetest of women, has an iron will that brooks no opposition in such matters. I went down on my knees beside Linda and took her in my arms. "Aw, honey," I told her, "if you want to give Mr. Riggs some mittens, you go right ahead!"

Every winter Jane made several pairs of zero-mittens for me. These were mittens cut from the best parts of my worn-out overalls, and lined with pieces of worn blankets. Then she would knit some cuffs of yarn, and sew them on.

These were the mittens Linda wanted to give to the old neighbor. Jane cut out two pairs for Old Man Riggs, but she left the sewing to Linda. She cut one pair from overalls, but she found an old skirt in the attic—I think the brightest red I ever saw—and she cut one pair from this. When they were finished, they went into a box, along with some of Jane's molasses cookies. Early on Christmas Eve, before dark, Linda took the box and left it on Riggs' porch.

About 11:00 next morning, my chores done, I was sitting in the living room, while Jane and Linda prepared our Christmas dinner. Suddenly, with a clatter like an earthquake in a tin shop, Old Man Riggs' Model T turned into our drive. He had his usual death grip on the wheel, but on his hands were the flaming red mittens!

He came to an abrupt halt just in front of the house and climbed painfully to the ground. He further mystified me by lifting a big cardboard grocery box from the rear seat. Then he marched right up to the front door, and knocked, holding the box under his arm. After the briefest of greetings, he asked for Linda. When she came in from the kitchen, he put his hand into the box and lifted something out. There, beautiful to behold, was the beloved, fabulous blue coat!

Linda let out a cry of wild delight, and then, after the manner of womankind, she began to sob. Mr. Riggs put his hand caressingly on her head with remarkable gentleness. "You know," he said, "I had a little girl just like you, once, a long time ago. Only her hair was red." He tried to say more, but only his lips moved.

A moment later, Jane came in from the kitchen. And piling surprise upon surprise, Old Man Riggs again reached into his box. What he handed Jane was a hand-tooled leather bag that must have cost fully as much as the coat! Riggs turned to me. "I hope," he growled, "you won't mind if I give your wife a Christmas present, John."

It wasn't just a common courtesy that made me ask Riggs to stay for dinner. The old man began to stammer and make excuses. But Jane would have none of this. "Nonsense," she chided, "we've got plenty for everyone, and it'll be ready in just a little while. Anyway," she clinched her argument, "I've already set a place for you."

Poor though we were, we never went hungry. The farm yielded an abundance of food, and it was nourishing and good. And Jane was a cook who could make a feast out of the plainest fare. There wasn't a turkey, but there was a fat chicken from our flock, as well as a pair of rabbits I had shot the day before, served, of course, with plenty of Jane's good cornbread dressing. We didn't have tea or coffee, but there were cider and milk aplenty.

I could tell the old man enjoyed the meal. There was a kind of dreamy look in his eyes. Once he looked at Jane, sort of stammered, and then remarked, "A man sorter forgets about a woman's way with food, when he lives by himself."

After the meal, Riggs sat in the living room with me for awhile, smoking a pipeful of my home-grown tobacco. But finally he put on his coat and started toward the door. "Gotta be about my chores," he explained. Then suddenly he turned to me and said, "You know, John, there's a place down at the end of my field, where an old road used to go through. If you'll fence that off, and run your stock down over it—it won't cost you a dime."

As he slipped through the door, he waved his red mittens and said, "Merry Christmas, Linda! If you will bring your basket to my house, I'll fill it up with some of them pears for your folks."

The Promise of the Doll

Ruth C. Ikerman

The act of giving ennobles and changes us, no matter what our age—especially if the motivation is right and the giving represents real sacrifice on the giver's part. The following story, though short, delivers a powerful message.

WHEN I met my friend on the crowded street, she held out her hand to me and said, "I hope you can help me. I'm desperate." Wearily she explained, "I'm about to cry and it's all over a doll. I simply have to find this doll for my granddaughter."

As tears filled her eyes, I remembered the terrible shock we all had felt over the death of her daughter, who had been such a vivacious young mother until stricken several months before. The young husband was doing a fine job with the little girl, but it was on the grandmother that much of the burden of planning for good things remained. And this explained her Christmas errand.

"I blame myself entirely," she told me, "for not starting earlier, but I never thought it would be a problem to find one of these special dolls. Yet there is not one of this variety left in town."

I asked her, "Well, why can't you settle for another kind of doll?"

She shook her head. "One of the last things my daughter ever said to me before the pain got so bad was how sorry she was that she had refused to buy this doll for her little girl. She told me she had thought the child was too young for such a doll, and had refused to buy it for her birthday, supposing there were lots of occasions ahead when she could get it for her."

Then she told the rest of the story. The little girl had come to her mother's bedside and asked whether the doll might arrive at Christmastime. The young mother grasped the tiny hand in hers and said, "I promise you this for Christmas." Then she had asked her own mother to do this one thing: "Just make sure that my little girl gets that doll this Christmas."

Now my friend was about to fail in her mission. "It's all my fault," she kept repeating. "I waited until too late. It will take a miracle now."

Secretly I agreed, but I tried to keep up a polite facade of courage. "Maybe the child has forgotten, and will be happy with something else."

Grimly my friend replied, "*She* may forget, but I won't." We parted to go our separate ways.

With my mind only half on my shopping, I found the ribbon a neighbor wanted to finish a baby blanket she was making. A few minutes later I stopped at her door to leave the package and was invited inside.

Her two little girls sat on the floor, playing with their dolls. As I sat down, I noticed that one of the dolls was the same type my friend was seeking. Hopefully I asked, "Can you remember where you bought that doll?"

My neighbor gave me her warmhearted smile. "That's not a doll," she said, "she's a member of the family, and as near as I can see she probably was born and not made. She came to us by plane from a favorite aunt in the East."

So I told her that I had a friend who was searching frantically for such a doll for the little girl whose mother had passed away during the year. Apparently unaware of us, the two children played happily. The mother and I spoke in adult words about facing loss at the holiday time, and how much we wished we could help my friend.

Later when I got up to leave, the two little girls followed me to the door.

"Dolly is ready to leave, too," they told me. Sure enough, she was dressed in a red velveteen coat and hat with a white fur muff.

"Where is dolly going?" I asked.

They laughed happily. "With you, of course. You know where the lady lives, don't you—the one who needs the doll so bad?"

I started to tell them that of course I couldn't take this doll. Then I looked at their faces, happy in the moment of giving. If I say the wrong thing now, something within my heart warned, I may ruin their joy of giving for the rest of their lives. Silently I took the doll, fumbling with my car keys so they did not see the mist over my eyes.

Their mother asked, "Are you both sure you want to do this?" They answered, "Yes, we do . . ." The mother put her arms around them tenderly.

Later I rang the doorbell of my friend. "Don't ask me how I got it, for I can't talk just yet. The doll is a little smudgy, but the worn places are from kisses and maybe they won't show under the Christmas lights."

She fondled the doll as though it were made of precious metal. Tears of joy welled up in the woman's eyes when I finally was able to tell the story.

"How can I ever thank those children enough?" she asked.

"They already have received a blessing greater than anything you or I could give them," I told her. "I saw their faces when they offered me the doll to bring to you."

And it was true. In the moment of giving they had also received, in ways past our finding out. A miracle had taken place. A promise could be kept, linking here with there, in the eternal circle of love of which the great gift of Christmas itself is a part.

The Christmas of the Phonograph Records

Mari Sandoz

We forget just how recent modern home conveniences are. I read this story not long ago to an aunt of mine who came from the part of Nebraska where this true story is set. She remembered that things in her childhood were very little different from those recounted by Sandoz. We also forget how starved those on the frontier were for music. This narrative communicates better, perhaps, than any other story I have come across just what it was like for a music lover, transplanted from civilized society, to live on the frontier shortly after the turn of the century.

IT SEEMS to me that I remember it all quite clearly. The night was very cold, footsteps squeaking in the frozen snow that had lain on for over two weeks, the roads in our region practically unbroken. But now the holidays were coming and wagons had pushed out on the long miles to the railroad, with men enough to scoop a trail for each other through the deeper drifts.

My small brother and I had been asleep in our attic bed long enough to frost the cover of the feather tick at our faces, when there was a shouting in the road before the house, running steps, and then the sound of the broom handle thumping against the ceiling below us and Father booming out, "Get up! The phonograph is here!"

The phonograph! I stepped out on the coyote skin at our bed, jerked on my woolen stockings and my shoes, buttoning my dress as I slipped down the outside stairs in the fading moon. Lamplight was pouring from the open door in a cloud of freezing mist over the back end of a loaded wagon, with three neighbors easing great boxes off, Father limping back and forth, shouting "Don't break me my records!" his breath white around his dark beard.

Inside the house Mother was poking sticks of wood into the firebox of the cookstove, her eyes meeting mine for a moment, shining, her concern about the extravagance of a talking machine when we needed overshoes for our chilblains apparently forgotten. The three largest boxes were edged through the doorway and filled much of the kitchen-living room floor. The neighbors stomped their felt boots at the stove and held their hands over the hot lids while Father ripped at the boxes with his crowbar, the frozen nails squealing as they let go. First there was the machine, varnished oak, with a shining cylinder for the records, and then the horn, a great black, gilt-ribbed morning glory, and the crazy angled rod arm and chain to hold it in place.

By now a wagon full of young people from the Dutch community on Mirage Flats turned into our yard. At a school program they had heard about the Edison phonograph going out to Old Jules Sandoz. They trooped in at our door, piled their wraps in the leanto, and settled along the benches to wait.

Young Jule and James, the brothers next to me in age, were up, too, and watching Father throw excelsior aside, exposing a tight packing of round paper containers a little smaller than a middle-sized baking powder can, with more layers under these, and still more below. Father opened one and while I read out the instructions in my German-accented fifth-grade country school English, he slipped the brown wax cylinder on the machine, cranked the handle carefully, and set the needle down. Everybody waited, leaning forward. There was a rhythmic frying in the silence, and then a whispering of sound, soft and very, very far away.

It brought a murmur of disappointment and an escaping laugh, but gradually the whispers loudened into the sextet from *Lucia,* into what still seems to me the most beautiful singing in the world. We all clustered around, the visitors, 14, 15 by now, and Mother too, caught while pouring hot chocolate into cups, her long-handled pan still tilted in the air. Looking back I realize something of the meaning of the light in her face: the hunger for music she must have felt, coming from Switzerland, the country of music, to a western government claim. True, we sang old country songs in the evenings, she leading, teaching us all she knew, but plainly it had not been enough, really nothing.

By now almost everybody pushed up to the boxes to see what there was to play, or called out some title hopefully. My place in this was established from the start. I was to run the machine, play the two-minute records set before me. There were violin pieces for Father, among them "Alpine Violet" and "Mocking Bird" from the first box opened; "Any Rags," "Red Wing," and "I'm Trying so Hard to Forget You" for the young people; "Rabbit Hash" for my brothers, their own selection from the catalog; and Schubert's "Serenade" and "Die Kapelle" for Mother, with almost everyone laughing over "Casey at the Telephone," all except Father. He claimed he could not understand such broken English, he who gave even the rankest westernism a French pronunciation.

With the trail broken to the main bridge of the region, just below our house, and this Christmas Eve, there was considerable travel on the road, people passing most of the night. The lighted windows, the music, the gathering of teams and saddlehorses in the yard, and the sub-zero weather tolled them in to the weathered little frame house with its lean-to.

"You better set more yeast. We will have to bake again tomorrow," Mother told me as she cut into a *zopf,* one of the braids of coffee cake baked in tins as large as the circle of both her arms. This was the last of five planned to carry us into the middle of holiday week.

By now the phonograph had been moved to the top of the washstand in our parents' kalsomined bedroom, people sitting on the two double beds, on the round-topped trunk, and on benches carried in, some squatting on their heels along the wall. The little round boxes stood everywhere, on the dresser and on the board laid from there to the washstand and on the window sills, with more brought in to be played and Father still shouting over the music, "Don't break me my records!" Some were broken, the boxes slipping out of the unaccustomed or cold-stiffened hands, the brown wax perhaps already cracked by the railroad.

When the Edison Military Band started a gay, blaring galop, Mother looked in at the bedroom door, pleased. Then she noticed all the records spread out there and in the kitchen-living room behind her, and began to realize their number. "Three hundred!" she exclaimed in German, speaking angrily in Father's direction. "Looks to me like more than 3,000!"

Father scratched under his bearded chin, laughing slyly. "I added to the order," he admitted. He didn't say how many, nor that there were other brands besides the Edison here, including several hundred foreign recordings obtained through a Swiss friend in New York, at a stiff price.

Mother looked at him, her blue eyes tragic, as she could make them. "You paid nothing on the mortgage! All the $2,100 inheritance wasted on a talking machine!"

No, Father denied, puffing at his corncob pipe. Not all. But Mother knew him well. "You did not buy the overshoes for the children. You forgot everything except your stamp collection, your guns, and the phonograph!"

"The overshoes are coming. I got them cheaper on time, with the guns."

"More debts!" she accused bitterly, but before she could add to this, one of the young Swiss, Maier perhaps, or Paul Freye, grabbed her and, against the stubbornness of her feet, whirled her back into the kitchen in the galop from the Edison band. He raced Mother from door to stove and back again and around and around, so her blue calico skirts flew out and the anger died from her face. Her eyes began to shine in an excitement I had never seen in them, and I realize now, looking back, all the fun our mother missed in her working life, even in her childhood in the old country, and during the much harder years later.

That galop started the dancing. Hastily the table was pushed against the wall, boxes piled on top of it, the big ones dragged into the lean-to. Waltzes, two-steps, quadrilles, and schottisches were sorted out and set in a row ready for me to play while one of the men shaved a candle over the kitchen floor. There was room for only one set of square dancers but our bachelor neighbor, Charley Sears, called the turns with enthusiasm. The Peters girls, two school teachers, and several other young women whom I've forgotten were well outnumbered by the men, as is common in new communities. They waltzed, two-stepped, formed a double line for a Bohemian polka, or schottisched around the room, one couple close behind the other to, perhaps, "It Blew, Blew, Blew." Once Charley Sears grabbed my hand and drew me out to try a quadrille, towering over me as he swung me on the corner and guided me through the allemande left. My heart pounded in shyness and my home-made shoes compounded my awkwardness. Later, someone else dragged me out into a two-step, saying, "Like this: 'one, two; one, two.' Just let yourself go."

. . . Even Old Jules had to try a round polka, even with his foot crippled in a long-ago well accident. When he took his pipe out of his mouth, dropped it lighted into his pocket, and whirled Mother around several times we knew that this was a special occasion. Before this we had never seen him even put an arm around her.

After the boys had heard their selection again, and "The Preacher and the Bear," they fell asleep on the floor and were carried to their bed in the lean-to. Suddenly I remembered little Fritzlie alone in the attic, perhaps half frozen. I hurried up the slippery, frosted steps. He was crying, huddled together under the feather tick, cold and afraid, deserted by the cat, too, sleeping against the warm chimney. I brought the boy down, heavy bulk that he was, and laid him in with his brothers. By then the last people started to talk of leaving, but the moon clouded over, the night-dark roads winding and treacherous through the drifts. Still, those who had been to town must get home with the Christmas supplies and such presents as they could manage for their children when they awoke in the morning.

Toward dawn Father dug out "Sempach," a song of a heroic Swiss battle, in which one of Mother's ancestors fell, and "Andreas Hofer," of another national hero. Hiding her pleasure at these records, Mother hurried away. . . . I mixed up a triple batch of baking powder biscuits and set on the two-gallon coffee pot. When the sun glistened on the frosted snow, the last of the horses huddled together in our yard were on the road. By then, some freighters forced to camp out by an upset wagon came whipping their teams up the icy pitch from the Niobrara River and stopped in. Father was slumped in his chair, letting his pipe fall into his beard, but he looked up and recognized the men as from a ranch accused of driving out bona fide settlers. Instead of rising to order them off the place he merely said "How!" in the Plains greeting, and dropped back into his doze. Whenever the music stopped noticeably, he lifted his shaggy head, complaining, "Can't you keep the machine going?" even if I had my hands in the biscuits. "Play 'The Mocking Bird' again," he might order, or a couple of the expensive French records of pieces he had learned to play indifferently in the violin lessons of his boyhood in Neuchatel. He liked "Spring Song," too, and "La Paloma," an excellent mandolin rendition of *"Come, Ye Disconsolate,"* and several

German love songs he had learned from his sweetheart, in Zurich, who had not followed him to America.

Soon my three brothers were up again and calling for their favorites . . . , Fritzlie from the top of two catalogs piled on a chair shouting too, just to be heard. None of them missed the presents that we never expected on Christmas; besides, what could be finer than the phonograph?

While Mother fed our few cattle and the hogs, I worked at the big stack of dishes with one of the freighters to wipe them. Afterward I got away to the attic and slept a little, the music from below faint through my floating of dreams. Suddenly I awoke, remembering what day this was and that young Jule and I had hoped Father might go cottontail hunting in the canyons up the river and help us drag home a little pine tree. Christmas had become a time for a tree, even without presents, a tree and singing, with at least one new song learned.

I dressed and hurried down. Father was asleep and there were new people in the bedroom and in the kitchen too, talking about the wonder of music rolling steadily from the big horn. In our Swiss way we had prepared for the usual visitors during the holidays, with family friends on Christmas and surely some of the European home-seekers Father had settled on free land, as well as passers by just dropping in to get warm and perhaps be offered a cup of coffee or chocolate. . . . Early in the forenoon the Syrian peddler we called Solomon drew up in the yard with his high four-horse wagon. I remember him every time I see a picture of Krishna Menon—the tufted hair, the same lean yellowish face and long white teeth. Solomon liked to strike our place for Christmas because there might be customers around and besides there was no display of religion to make him uncomfortable in his Mohammedanism, Father said, although one might run into a stamp-collecting priest or a hungry preacher at our house almost any other time.

So far as I know, Solomon was the first to express what others must have thought. "Excuse it please, Mrs. Sandoz," he said, in the polite way of peddlers, "but it seem to uneducated man like me the new music is for fine palace—"

Father heard him. "Nothing's too good for my family and my neighbors," he roared out.

"The children have the frozen feet—" the man said quietly.

"Frozen feet heal! What you put in the mind lasts!"

The peddler looked down into his coffee cup, half full of sugar, and said no more.

It was true that we had always been money poor and plainly would go on so, but there was plenty of meat and game, plenty of everything that the garden, the young orchard, the field, and the open country could provide, and for all of which there was no available market. Our bread, dark and heavy, was from our hard macaroni wheat ground at a local water mill . . . , the cellar full of our own potatoes, barrels of pickles and sauerkraut, and hundreds of jars of canned fruit and vegetables, crocks of jams and jellies, wild and tame, including buffalo berry, that wonderful tart, golden-red jelly from the silvery bush that seems to retreat before close settlement much like the buffalo and whooping crane. Most of the root crops were in a long pit outside, and the attic was strung with little sacks of herbs and polly seeds, bigger ones of dried green beans, sweet corn, chokecherries, sandcherries, and wild plums. Piled along the low sides of the attic were bushel bags of popcorn, peas, beans, and lentils, the flour stacked in rows with room between for the mousing cat.

Sugar, coffee, and chocolate were practically all we bought for the table, with perhaps a barrel of blackstrap molasses for cookies and brown cake, all laid in while the fall roads were still open.

When the new batch of coffee cake was done and the fresh bread and buns, the goose in the oven, we took turns getting scrubbed at the heater in the leanto, and put on our best clothes, mostly made over from some adult's but well sewn. Finally we spread Mother's two old country linen cloths over the table for 22 places. While Mother passed the platters, I fed the phonograph with records that Mrs. Surber and her three musical daughters had selected, soothing music: Bach, Mozart, Brahms, and *"Moonlight Sonata"* on two foreign records that Father had hidden away so they would not be broken, along with an a capella *"Stille Nacht"* and some other foreign ones

Mother wanted saved. For lightness, Mrs. Surber had added "The Last Rose of Summer," to please Elsa, the young soprano soon to be a professional singer in Cleveland, and a little Strauss and Puccini, while the young people wanted Ada Jones and "Monkey Land" by Collins and Harlan.

There was stuffed Canada goose with the buffalo berry jelly; . . . watercress salad; chow-chow and pickles, sweet and sour; dried green beans cooked with . . . a hint of garlic; carrots, turnips, mashed potatoes and gravy, with coffee from the start to the pie, pumpkin and gooseberry. At the dishpan set on the high water bench, where I had to stand on a little box for comfort, the dishes were washed as fast as they came off the table, with a relay of wipers. There were also waiting young men and boys to draw water from the bucket well, to chop stove wood and carry it in.

As I recall now, there were people at the table for hours. A letter of Mother's says that the later uninvited guests got sausage and sauerkraut, squash, potatoes and fresh bread, with canned plums and cookies for dessert. Still later there was a big roaster full of beans and sidemeat brought in by a lady homesteader, and some mince pies made with wild plums to lend tartness instead of apples, which cost money.

All this time there was the steady stream of music and talk from the bedroom. I managed to slip in the "Lucia" a couple of times until a tart-tongued woman from over east said she believed I was getting addled from all that hollering. We were not allowed to talk back to adults, so I put on the next record set before me, this one "Don't Get Married Any More, Ma," selected for a visiting Chicago widow looking for her fourth husband, or perhaps her fifth. Mother rolled her eyes up at this bad taste, but Father and the other old-timers laughed over their pipes.

We finally got Mother off to bed in the attic for her first nap since the records came. Downstairs the floor was cleared and the Surber girls showed their dancing-school elegance in the waltzes. There was a stream of young people later in the afternoon, many from the skating party at the bridge. Father, red-eyed like the rest of us, limped among them, soaking up their praise, their new respect. By this time my brothers and I had given up having a tree. Then a big boy from up the river rode into the yard dragging a pine behind his horse. It was a shapely tree, and small enough to fit on a box in the window, out of the way. The youth was the son of Father's worst enemy, the man who had sworn in court that Jules Sandoz shot at him, and got our father 30 days in jail, although everybody, including the judge, knew that Jules Sandoz was a crack shot and what he fired at made no further appearances.

As the son came in with the tree, someone announced loudly who he was. I saw Father look toward his Winchester on the wall, but he was not the man to quarrel with an enemy's children. Then he was told that the boy's father himself was in the yard. Now Jules Sandoz paled above his bearding, paled so the dancers stopped, the room silent under the suddenly foolish noise of the big-horned machine. Helpless, I watched Father jump toward the rifle. Then he turned, looked to the man's gaunt-faced young son.

"Tell your old man to come in. We got some good Austrian music."

So the man came in, and sat hunched over near the door. Father had left the room, gone to the leanto, but after a while he came out, said his "How!" to the man, and paid no attention while Mrs. Surber pushed me forward to make the proper thanks for the tree that we were starting to trim as usual. We played "The Blue Danube" and some other pieces long forgotten now for the man, and passed him the coffee and *kuchli* with the others. He tasted the thin flaky frycakes. "Your mother is a good cook," he told me. "A fine woman."

When he left with the skaters all of Father's friends began to talk at once, fast, relieved. "You could have shot him down, on your own place, and not got a day in the pen for it," one said.

Old Jules nodded. "I got no use for his whole outfit, but the music is for everybody."

As I recall now, perhaps half a dozen of us, all children, worked at the tree, looping my strings of red rose hips and popcorn around it, hanging the people and animal cookies with chokecherry eyes, distributing the few Christmas tree balls and the tinsel and candleholders that the Surbers had given us several years before. I brought out the boxes of candles I had made by dipping string in melted tallow, and then we lit the candles and with my schoolmates I ran out into the cold of the road to look. The tree showed fine through the glass.

Now I had to go to bed, although the room below me was alive with dancing and I remembered that Jule and I had not sung our new song, "Amerika ist ein schones Land," at the tree.

Holiday week was much like Christmas, the house full of visitors as the news of the fine music and the funny records spread. People appeared from 50, 60 miles away and farther so long as the new snow held off, for there was no other such collection of records in all of western Nebraska, and none with such an open door. There was something for everybody, Irishmen, Scots, Swedes, Danes, Poles, Czechs, as well as the Germans and the rest, something pleasant and nostalgic. The greatest variety in tastes was among the Americans, from "Everybody Works but Father," "Arkansas Traveler," and "Finkelstein at the Seashore," to love songs and the sentimental "Always in the Way"; from home and native region pieces to the patriotic and religious. They had strong dislikes too, even in war songs. One settler, a GAR veteran, burst into tears and fled from the house at the first notes of "Tenting Tonight." Perhaps it was the memories it awakened. Many Americans were as interested in classical music as any European, and it wasn't always a matter of cultivated taste. One illiterate little woman from down the river cried with joy at Rubinstein's "Melody in F."

"I has heard me talkin' and singin' before," she said apologetically as she wiped her eyes, "but I wasn't knowin' there could be something sweet as that come from a horn."

Afternoons and evenings, however, were still the time for the dancers. Finally it was New Year, the day when the Sandoz relatives, siblings, uncles and cousins, gathered, perhaps 20 of them immigrants brought in by the land locator, Jules. This year they were only a sort of eddy in the regular stream of outsiders. Instead of nostalgic jokes and talk of the family and the old country, there were the records to hear, particularly the foreign ones, and the melodies of the old violin lessons that the brothers had taken, and the guitar and mandolin of their one sister. Jules had to endure a certain amount of joking over the way he spent most of his inheritance. One brother was building a cement block home in place of his soddy with his, and a greenhouse. The sister was to have a fine large barn instead of a new home because her husband believed that next year Halley's comet would bring the end of the world. Ferdinand, the youngest of the brothers, had put his money into wild-cat oil stock and planned to become very wealthy.

Although most of their talk was in French, which Mother did not speak, they tried to make up for this by complimenting her on the excellence of her chocolate and her golden fruit cake. Then they were gone, hot bricks at their feet, and calling back their adieus from the freezing night. It was a good thing they left early, Mother told me. She had used up the last of the chocolate, the last cake of the 25-pound caddies. We had baked up two sacks of flour, 49 pounds each, in addition to all that went into the Christmas preparations before the phonograph came. Three-quarters of a 100-pound bag of coffee had been roasted, ground and used during the week. . . . The floor of the kitchen-living room, old and worn anyway, was much thinner for the week of dancing. New Year's night a man who had been there every day, all week, tilted back on one of the kitchen chairs and went clear through the floor.

"Oh, the fools!" Father shouted at us all. "Had to wear out my floor dancing!"

But plainly he was pleased. It was a fine story to tell for years, all the story of the phonograph records. He was particularly gratified by the praise of those who knew something about music, people like the Surbers and a visitor from a Czech community, a relative of Dvorak, the great composer. The man wrote an item for the papers, saying, "This Jules Sandoz has not only settled a good community of homeseekers, but is enriching their cultural life with the greatest music of the world."

"Probably wants to borrow money from you," Mother said. "He has come to the wrong door."

Gradually the records for special occasions and people were stored in the lean-to. For those used regularly, Father and a neighbor made a lot of flat boxes to fit under the beds, always handy, and a cabinet for the corner at the bedroom door. The best,

the finest from both the Edison and the foreign recordings, were put into this cabinet, with a door that didn't stay closed. One warmish day when I was left alone with the smaller children, the water pail needed refilling. I ran out to draw a bucket from the well. It was a hard and heavy pull for a growing girl and I hated it, always afraid that I wouldn't last and would have to let the rope slip and break the windlass.

Somehow, in my uneasy hurry, I left the door ajar. The wind blew it back and when I had the bucket started up the 65-foot well, our big old sow, loose in the yard, pushed her way into the house. Horrified, I shouted to Fritzlie to get out of her way, but I had to keep pulling and puffing until the bucket was at the top. Then I ran in. Fritzlie was up on a chair, safe, but the sow had knocked down the record cabinet and scattered the cylinders over the floor. Standing among them as in corn, she was chomping down the wax records that had rolled out of the boxes, eating some, box and all. Furiously I thrashed her out with the broom, amidst squealings and shouts. Then I tried to save what I could. The sow had broken at least 30 or 35 of the best records and eaten all or part of 20 more. "La Paloma" was gone, and "Traumerei" and "Spring Song"; "Evening Star," too, and half of "Moonlight Sonata" and many others, foreign and domestic, including all of Brahms.

I got the worst whipping of my life for my carelessness, but the loss of the records hurt more, and much, much longer.

Guest in the House

Ruth Emery Amanrude

It takes many of us a lifetime to learn these simple lessons: we should be real, we should be genuine, and we should share with others the things and traditions and people that are dear and meaningful to us. This particular story has long been one of our family's favorites, for it cuts right through our formalities to the heart of the Christmas season, to the essence of the holiday: the celebration once again of the birth, life, death, and resurrection of our Lord.

JOE'S reaction to the pink Christmas tree was a flat and stubborn "No!" And she had been doing it all for him, too, just so they could make a nice impression on the Widdams, but that Joe was such a stick-in-the-mud.

Edie had started to plan the special Christmas Eve the night Joe first told her he wanted Clarice and Ed Widdam for Christmas. Even while she was protesting that the house was too small and too plain to entertain their sophisticated new neighbors, she was working on her list.

She *had* to make a good impression. The Widdams were obviously people who did things the right way. Their new rambler house was the ramblingest in the neighborhood; their attached garage held two shining cars. Just meeting smartly dressed Clarice Widdam in the supermarket made Edie feel all helter-skelter and almost dowdy. And Joe wanted the Widdams for Christmas Eve.

"They were tickled, honey," Joe told Edie when she reminded him again that their own Collins family Christmas was so old-fashioned. "This is their first Christmas here since Ed was transferred, and they haven't been here long enough to really know anybody. And Ed loves kids, Edie! He even wants to help out coaching one of the kid baseball teams this summer."

"Oh, goody," Edie said bitingly, "that's how we'll entertain them, then. We'll have a ball game. With Uncle Maynard and Aunt Helen and Cousin Fred, we'll have just enough for a team!" Edie was furious with Joe. Any other time she would have been delighted—but Christmas!

There would be Uncle Maynard and Aunt Helen, each with the latest in aches and pains and their respective remedies. Joe's cousin, Fred, a most uninteresting but kindly soul, would come with his drugstore-wrapped parcels and his wordy explanations of why the large-sized colognes were really the practical buy. The children would be wound up like tops and every good manner and really natural charm would be lost in the mix-up.

Everything for Edie started with a list, so she wrote down every detail of a simple but charmingly served dinner. She planned the children's time so they would not get out of hand. She had revised, rewritten, replanned, and reorganized until the list was perfect. And now she couldn't find it!

"Where did I put it?" she asked herself desperately as she ransacked all the known tuck-away places in the house. Maybe the children would know. They certainly could find anything else that was hidden away.

"Connie!" Edie really didn't expect an answer, because 11-year-old Connie had a deafness that could be turned on and off according to the tone of her mother's voice. Today she responded promptly and she trailed in dragging four feet of shower curtain behind her.

"Connie, what in the world are you supposed to be?" Again expecting no answer, Edie went on, "Have you seen my list?"

"Which one?" Connie asked absently as she posed before the wall mirror. "What list are you talking about?"

"The list of things to do for Christmas. I can't find anything in this clutter."

The living room did have that Friday-afternoon look, plus a little extra disorder of the rewrapped gift parcels brought home from school parties. This was the Friday before Christmas, but more important to Edie, it was the Friday before Widdams!

"I see Bill has been home, too," Edie muttered, glancing at a pair of ice skates, a wad of damp towels, and something that looked like a rusty trap lying just inside the living room door. "To him, home is just one big closet."

"Billy's walking a girl home," giggled Connie, now completely swathed in shower curtain.

"That's nice," Edie drawled. "I hope she inspires him to comb his hair and tuck in his shirttail."

"She's drippy, and so is Bill." Now Connie had one of Edie's brass candlesticks aloft in one hand.

"OK, Connie, I give up! What are you, the Statue of Liberty?"

"Mother! Don't you know a Wise Man when you see one?" Connie was shocked with her mother's lack of appreciation.

"Nope, I guess not! I don't get to meet many wise men—not lately, anyway."

"This is a *Bible* Wise Man! It's for the church play! You forgot!"

Oh, dear, I almost did, Edie thought, but she said, "Not really, dear. Do you know your part?"

"Mine and everyone else's, too," retorted Connie in the know-it-all tone that Edie found unbearable at times. "Is this how a Wise Man should look, Mom?"

"Exactly, dear, and now please *be* one and remember where you saw the list."

"I saw it in your hand, that's where, and I think it's silly. A list for what we do at Christmas! We always do the same things!" Now she was Connie again, and the shower curtain was just a shower curtain.

That's just the trouble, thought Edie, *we always do the same things*. But this year *had* to be different. She'd *have* to make a new list, that's all.

The sound of the piano in the playroom started. "Oh, no," she groaned, "not that again!"

Two months ago, 8-year-old Carol had balked like a young mule at every reminder to practice her piano lessons. Suddenly, it was different. She had burst into the house two weeks ago, brown eyes shining, crying, "I have a special piece! For two hands! With runs 'n' everything!"

To Edie, Carol's lessons proved no musical ability, merely showed her to be ambidextrous, with her left and right hands working completely independent of each other. Sometimes Edie was sure they were playing two different pieces. But Carol plugged along, counting her one-and-ah, two-and-ah's almost as loudly as she played those unmatched notes. Today it was *too* much.

"Carol! Carol, please!" Edie had to wait for the two-and-ah before she could be heard. Surprisingly, Carol's square little figure appeared promptly.

"Hi, Mom. Where you been? We had a party at school, and we each got a autograph book from Miss Buckley, and we brought home our decorations for our own tree!"

And there they were, wrapped in her sturdy little arms—yards and yards of orange-red paper links! Oh, no, thought Edie, not *orange!*

"They're very pretty, honey," Edie said evenly, "but wouldn't you like to have them in the playroom instead?"

"Oh, no, Mom! They're for everyone, not just me! Connie has so many more things on the tree than I do."

Carol's voice told how much the crudely made chain meant to her, and Edie could picture the dark, shining head bent over the task of making this "for everyone."

"Of course, honey. We'll keep it with all the other Christmas things." Edie resolved to find some place for the chain, Widdams or no Widdams.

The big box taken from the storage closet each year held a wealth of these treasures, each marked carefully: "Billy, first grade," or "Connie, kindergarten," and so on. Each Christmas found the keepsakes a little more worn and defaced but a little more precious.

The box presented a real problem for Edie this year, because the first item on her list had been the pink Christmas tree. That's when Joe shot sparks.

"Whoever heard of a pink Christmas tree!" His nice, Irishy face was anything but nice right then. "Listen, Edie, the Widdams are coming here to spend *our* Christmas in *our* way. That does not include a pink Christmas tree!"

"Oh, Joe, just once can't we do something with a

little flair to it?" Edie begged. Joe was unmovable.

"Honey, you can flair all over the place, but you know the kids have had their eyes on a tree in Carlson's woods for a long time. The tree-chopping trip is a part of Christmas, and the kids love it. And so do I. No pink Christmas tree!"

"All right, then. Be stubborn. You know I'm planning everything just for the Widdams." Her voice was at the near-tear stage, and her cheeks were flushed.

"Well, my pet, you can *un*plan everything, then. It's Christmas the old way." And Joe's voice said that ended that.

So it was going to be the regular, ordinary green Christmas tree with Connie's kindergarten angel and Bill's lopsided stars made from tin-can covers and Carol's orange-red chain and all the other off-colored contributions with their dabs of paste and fingerprints still showing.

It isn't that we'd never use them again, Edie's conscience whispered. It's just that this year was to be so special!

Joe shot more sparks over the menu. "What do you mean, roast beef?" he asked as he read the list over her shoulder. "What's the matter with *lutfisk*?"

"But, Joe, you never liked *lutfisk* when we were first married," Edie protested. "And the smell!"

"Well, I like it now—smell and all!" Joe's voice softened as he went on. "As far as not liking it, honey, it was just that it was new to me. I never had any Christmas traditions until you showed me.

Christmas dinner off a menu, that's what I had. And now *lutfisk* is part of our Christmas."

Edie felt a little ashamed because she remembered too that Joe, who had lived in a succession of rooming houses with his widowed father, had never known the warmth of a family Christmas until their marriage. She had loved his delight and surprise as each new tradition had been introduced, and she had felt a little proud that she could bring a real Christmas feeling into his life.

So, the list had been changed: Green Christmas tree. *Lutfisk*.

A banging in the hall interrupted her thoughts. Bill's half-bass, half-treble voice called out, "We're home!"

"You're telling me," she muttered, but she called, "Welcome! You can start in by putting away your share of the loot stowed around here!"

"You sound crabby, Mom," Bill said, as he added a cap and jacket to the mound on the floor.

"I'm in a boy-eating mood, my lad, so do as you're told. You, too," she added as she helped 5-year-old Rog with his snowsuit.

Oh, dear, she thought as they went up the stairs. *Don't let me get owly over this.*

Friday night was meeting night for everyone but Edie and Rog, so after his bath and story and prayers and three drinks of water, plus a last minute summons to ask if "Santa Claus had any *real* children of his own," Edie was alone. By the time Joe and the

74

children came home, the new list was ready, and there wasn't a thing on it to get excited about. It'll be the same old Christmas to us, but the *lutfisk* and the decorations will probably make it the most unusual one the Widdams ever spent, Edie thought grimly, as she tumbled into bed beside the sleeping Joe.

Early Saturday morning, Joe and the children went after the tree. Back in two hours, singing noisily, they tramped through the house like a parade. Then the whole family had a hand in decorating. Though Edie pitched in reluctantly, she soon was giggling with the rest over the yield of the treasure box.

"Pretty crummy looking stable," Bill muttered, but his face shone at the family's staunch denials.

Just let that Clarice Widdam look down her nose at it! Edie thought. Bill placed the crudely carved lamb and burro in front of the stable he had made from wooden cheese boxes.

"Here's my angel! Where does it go?" squealed Connie.

"Same place as always, hon," Joe told her. "Right on top." And he reached up to place the faded and wilting angel in the uppermost branch.

Next came Bill's stars and Carol's orange-red chain, and then round-eyed Rog cried, "My twinklers!" and Edie helped him to reach up with his paper spirals that bounced like springs and really did twinkle with bits of sequins.

One by one, the treasures were discovered anew. The *tomte gabbe* — and Edie was touched to hear Joe tell Rog that this was *not* Santa Claus but a little elf that Edie's mother, Grandma Hanson, had brought from Sweden. The *jul bok*, raggedy now and brittle, but again Edie had to tell the story of how in Sweden every home has a large straw goat in the yard during the holiday season. A space was cleared on the mantle for the *angla spel*, and after the brass was polished, Connie set the four little candles in place, and Joe touched a match to each wick. The *angla spel* was a favorite with the children, and they loved to watch as the heat of the candle flames started the four chubby angels spinning round and round, each with a wand that touched a little brass chime. "Now it *sounds* like Christmas, too," Carol breathed ecstatically.

Then Joe snapped the switch for the lights. "Oh," breathed the children in unison, as the soft blues and reds and golds of the tiny lamps were reflected in the shimmering tinsel. "It's the most beautiful tree ever!" *It is pretty*, Edie thought, *but I did want a pink one with silver ornaments!*

Sunday brought Aunt Helen, complete with cold tablets and liniment and worn out from her bus trip from Duluth. Once Uncle Maynard appeared, though, she fell into a lively swap of symptoms that brought a healthy glow to her eyes. She was not to be outdone; whatever ailment he named, she had one more serious!

At least I don't have to worry about entertaining

them, thought Edie. *But the Widdams will get one look at us and one whiff of that* lutfisk *plus Aunt Helen's liniment, and they'll think we came over on the last boat!*

Cousin Fred, always a favorite with the children, arrived with his pockets bulging and his red face wreathed in smiles, and quickly escaped to the play-room where the racket became almost unbearable. Even Joe, who had stoutly defended Carol's musical ability, finally begged her to stop. "You'd think she could play something besides that tune," he complained cheerfully, as a loud "one-and-ah" was accompanied by a halting run.

Rog darted in and out on mysterious errands. A rope. A knife. Connie wanted to borrow Edie's coral beads. Bill *needed* a flashlight. And so the day went, and suddenly it was Monday and the day of Christmas Eve. The day of the Widdams.

"This one day should have 24 hours all between lunch and dinner," Edie said as she rushed through the house. She scarcely had the last bit of holly tacked in place when the Widdams arrived.

Ed Widdam was hearty and friendly, and the children took him over at once. Clarice Widdam smiled sweetly and thanked Edie for allowing them to come. "I told Ed it was almost too much to expect," she said in her soft voice, "but I think the idea of having children around at Christmas was a temptation that overcame his good manners."

"Oh, but we *wanted* you," Edie replied eagerly, and she found herself meaning it.

Clarice was generous in her compliments about the house and the children, and she won Aunt Helen completely with her sympathy. *She's a lady, all right,* Edie thought.

Everything went well, and Joe beamed with pride as the children pointed out the treasures on the tree. "The twinklers are mine," Rog told them proudly, "but they're for everyone."

"And I made the chain," Carol added, "and Connie made the angel when she was only 6 years old."

"Such a Christmasy angel, too," Clarice Widdam said.

"I'll have to make a new manger next year," Bill said in his half-man voice, and making an awkward attempt to explain the crude stable.

"But you must always keep this one, Bill," Clarice told him. "It's the very first one you made; that makes it special." Edie thanked her silently with her eyes.

The room looked like Christmas. The little *angla spel* tinkled away merrily and the festive glow of the tree shone on the happy faces in the room.

Suddenly Clarice Widdam exclaimed, "What *is* that I smell?"

Edie's heart went plop! *I knew it*, she thought. *Here goes our nice impression!*

"It's *lutfisk*," Joe said. And he made it sound like pheasant under glass. "We have it every year. It's Scandinavian, you know."

"Indeed I do know," answered Clarice, "and it's years since I've had it." At Edie's look of surprise, Clarice continued, "I'm one of those Minnesota Swedes you hear about, and I used to see the *lutfisk* stacked like cord wood outside my father's grocery store. The weather would be cold enough to keep it until it was taken home and soaked for hours. Then it was trimmed and tied in a cheesecloth bag and cooked in a huge kettle and soon we'd smell it all over the house. That wonderful, wonderful smell!"

Edie felt weak. *And I was for beef*, she thought. "I'm so glad you like it. For us, it wouldn't be Christmas without *lutfisk*—even my big Irishman loves it." And from her big Irishman she received a wry and slightly accusing grin that made her squirm.

"And who wouldn't like it?" asked Clarice, daring anyone to speak up.

Aunt Helen, rejuvenated by the thought of food, added, "And it's so healthy. So easy to digest." Uncle Maynard just nodded and Cousin Fred beamed and said the way he liked *lutfisk* was in large quantities.

And so dinner was a wonderful success. The chatter was gay and familyish, and the Widdams obviously enjoyed everything and everybody. As they left the table, Clarice Widdam said, "This is a Christmas I shall never forget. It is almost as though it were planned just for me."

It was, thought Edie, avoiding Joe's look—*for you, in spite of me and my big ideas.*

"It's time for the program!" sang out Rog, as the family and guests settled themselves in the living room.

Every Christmas Eve, right after dinner and before any gifts were opened, the family sang carols and the children performed their parts from the church and school programs. Edie had hoped to postpone this little ceremony until after the guests' departure, and now she murmured, almost apologetically, "They love this part of Christmas."

"Why, of course they do," Clarice's eyes were sparkling and she applauded softly, encouraging the children to begin.

After a few minutes of whispered conference in the hall, Bill entered with a wooden box that he placed carefully at one end of the room. His back was turned, but when he moved aside, they could see the shaded glow of light that came from inside the box.

"It's a cradle," whispered Clarice. "They've made a cradle for their program."

So that's why they wanted a flashlight, Edie thought.

Bill left quietly, and serious little Rog entered. In childish, measured tones he recited his Sunday-school "Welcome One and All" poem and bowed formally during the applause that followed. Still un-smiling, Rog announced. "In a minute, we'll have a play—soon's I put my costume on. I have *two* parts, because there aren't enough of us to *be* everything." He did smile then, but a sibilant whisper from the hall restored his dignity and he went on. "The people in the play are Miss Constance Collins; she's the Wise Man. Mr. William Collins is the shepherd, and I am—and Mr. Roger Collins is—the angel." At that moment he looked like one. "Miss Carol Collins is the accompa—she plays the piano." He started to leave, but hesitated long enough to say, "We all wrote the play, only Connie did the most."

There was a little flurry of excitement in the hall, and then Carol entered and seated herself with dignity at the piano. She played a halting arrangement of "Silent Night" as the others came in. Connie, resplendent in the shower curtain and with Edie's coral beads holding a silk scarf on her head, led the procession. Thought Edie, *It really doesn't look like a shower curtain now.* In her hands Connie held a long white scroll, and on her face was a look of reverence.

Next came Bill in Joe's striped bathrobe tied with a stout rope around his slim waist. His head was hooded and he carried Carol's old toy lamb under his arm. Rog came last, swathed in white, with two huge paper wings pinned to his back. On his head was a band of tinsel. As he took his place behind the cradle, the glow from within gave an added radiance to his sweet face and made the tinsel band truly a halo.

Connie read the Christmas story from her scroll. The children stood quietly, moving only as the lovely story progressed. They looked at the sky and at the Star everyone felt was really there. They expressed the awe of the shepherds and the Wise Men. They knelt in adoration before the Manger of the Babe.

And then the piano started again. Edie sat straight and stiff as she recognized the long-practiced melody and she groped for Joe's hand. Carol's fingers seemed so sure, and though her lips counted the one-and-ah, two-and-ah's, she did not miss a note.

Forgive me, Edie thought. *They knew all the time what was really important about Christmas and I almost forgot. To think they had to show me again! It isn't pink Christmas trees or something you can put on a list. It isn't glitter and impressions. It's all this—love and sweetness and sharing.* She felt the understanding pressure of Joe's hand on hers, and with her eyes filled with happy tears, she listened to the children sing.

Sweetly and simply, their voices rang out in the words. "Happy Birthday to You. Happy Birthday to You. Happy Birthday, Dear Jesus, Happy Birthday to You."

Gift for David

Lon Woodrum

Terminal illness is almost always heartbreaking, but when such a tragedy happens to a child at Christmas it is triply so. As for miracles, we are programmed to believe that they occurred only in "olden times"—certainly not in today's mechanized society. But this moving story reminds us that God remains God.

SUCH a thing hasn't happened often, I suppose. But it did happen in Springfield that Christmas. And I'm not the only one who can tell you about it. Dr. Wallis Martin knows the facts. And so does Dr. Gaffel, the specialist. And Mrs. Carol Devoe will vouch for it, too.

Frank Gammon, editor of the *Daily Eagle* and my boss, called me into his office that day and held out a slip of paper.

"Look, Al. Run this down," he said. "Kid dying of leukemia. Won't live till Christmas, but he's all set to celebrate. Sounds like a story."

You don't mind the Old Man's blunt words. It was just his way. We all knew he liked kids. I took the slip of paper and left the office. The slip said, "David Stone. Mother: Carol Stone. 1745 Elm Street."

I went out on the street. A few big snowflakes drifted down on the still air like tiny white paratroopers. From the courthouse tower Christmas music floated over Springfield.

Driving down Sheridan, I passed Calvary Church, where I was a member. I saw my pastor, Allan Comer, going up the church steps and waved at him. Wonderful fellow, that. He had shown me the way to a new life in Christ.

I stopped my car at a white frame house. There was a small Christmas tree in the window. I rang the bell, and the door was opened by a woman who looked a little younger than myself, around 30, with sea-colored eyes and dark hair drawn back from an intelligent, pretty face. She had a full mouth and was slim and nearly as tall as my own five feet eleven.

"I'm Al Devoe from the *Daily Eagle*," I said. "I'd like to have a talk with David Stone, if I may. Are you Mrs. Stone?"

"Yes," she said. "Why do you want to see him?"

"Our editor asked me to come. May I see him?"

She hesitated. "I don't want his sufferings smeared all over the papers."

"I'll handle the story properly, Mrs. Stone."

I kept looking at her. Her pale skin stood out against her dark hair and her eyes were rather a contrast to both. Her eyes interested me. They were cold, yet they were trying to be warm! Something besides her son's illness seemed to be needling her.

She led me into a bedroom to a boy propped up on pillows. He was about 10. The little fellow grinned at me and said, "Hi, mister. Merry Christmas!"

I tossed my hat on the bed. "I'm Al Devoe, Dave. How's things?"

"Things are just fine," he said, "even if I have to be in bed a few days."

I glanced up and saw pain catch at the mother's face. She turned away from me. I said to David, "Are you looking forward to Christmas?"

"Sure!" He grinned. "It's a time for us to remember God's birthday."

"Jesus' birthday. Some people don't think of that fact first when they talk about Christmas."

"I believe in Jesus. Mother doesn't believe in Him, but I do."

Again I glanced at Carol Stone, but she did not look at me. She went out of the bedroom.

"Why doesn't your mother believe in Jesus?" I asked gently.

"Oh, she just doesn't. I can't make her understand."

He paused and squinted at me. "Maybe you could help me make her understand." He seemed to take it for granted that I was a Christian.

I reached out and patted his slim shoulder.

"Maybe I might do that, pal. Tell me, do you mind being in bed at Christmas?"

"Oh, it's not Christmas yet. Not quite. I'll be well by Christmas!"

I gazed at him. His dark eyes were like two bright stars in his pallid face. "Well, that's swell, Dave. It really is."

"I have faith in God," he said simply.

This, I thought, *is quite a story!*

In the living room I found Carol Stone gazing out a window. She turned and said, "I can't bear all his brave talk about getting well by Christmas. Dr. Martin says there is no chance."

"Faith," I said, "can sometimes do strange things."

"Faith!" Harshness covered the softness of her voice. She lifted a slim hand. "It sounds so well as a word. But it's pretty meaningless, really."

I concentrated on her. "You've had it rough, huh?"

"Are you a reporter or a preacher?"

"A reporter, but I wouldn't mind being a preacher. I think it's a great calling."

She shrugged. Bitterness hardened a mouth that wanted to be tender.

"Don't preach here! I couldn't bear it."

She sounded as if she might cry, and I said, "I'm sorry I've disturbed you, Mrs. Stone."

She shook her head. "Oh, it's all right. I'm just upset. Not over you."

"The boy's father?" I ventured, and stopped.

She put a quick look on me and took a deep breath. "David had a father, of course. I was married to him for four years. He was a religious man—very religious!" She smiled sardonically. "He ran off with a religious woman!"

"Oh! I'm sorry. But some religious people just aren't Christians, you know."

She melted a little. She needed to talk. "I've had a difficult time looking after David. I had a job—with the American Insurance Company. But David's illness . . ." She went to the coffee table for her purse and took out a handkerchief.

"His father never came to see him?"

"His father is dead. He was killed in an automobile wreck. David doesn't remember him. And I'm glad he doesn't."

I twisted my hat brim in my hands. "Life can be hard at times. But it takes a faith like David's to be equal to it."

"Poor little fellow! He's so sweet—and so deceived! He really thinks he'll get well. He doesn't even know what leukemia is!"

I went to the door. "If I can do anything, let me know," I said.

She nodded but didn't say anything. I went to my car with David's face before me. And his mother's, too. The face of faith and the face of doubt, side by side.

Back at the *Daily Eagle* I got a photographer to go out for a picture of David. Then I beat out the story. It ran the next day in the *Eagle*. The day following it was picked up and flashed all over the country by the press. There were even a few editorials on it. Television and radio took it up, too.

The Old Man sent me out for a follow-up story, and, brother, when I got out there! You never saw so many gifts pouring into one place. Packages— big, little, and medium-sized. I waded through them into the bedroom, and there in the midst of more toys beamed a pale-faced David.

"Boy," he said, "everybody is wishing me a happy Christmas!"

"You've gotten to be an important fellow," I said.

He grinned hugely. "People care when you're sick, don't they?"

I stiffened, and looked quickly at his mother. *Sick! The people think you're going to die, Davy! They love you when they think you're going to die!* A vast sadness washed through me, and for a moment I must have shared some of his mother's feelings.

In the living room she said, "I don't think I can bear it."

"Because people have proved their sympathy for a boy like David? At least this proves everybody isn't like the guy who has made you so bitter."

Her eyes narrowed. "It proves nothing except that people are sentimental and swayed by publicity! I wish I hadn't let you run the story in the paper. I can't stand it—seeing all those gifts pouring in for a boy who'll never live to enjoy them. If people were human they'd give to the living, not to the dead!"

"Listen—"

"David had so little when he was well and able to run about. No father, sometimes barely enough to eat. Now, when he's bound to a deathbed, things come in a flood! It's all so—so stupid!"

I left and went to the office of Dr. Wallis Martin. I knew him quite well, and he saw me.

"The boy has leukemia, Al," the doctor said. "I made sure about it. I consulted with Dr. Gaffel, a top man in this field. The diagnosis is certain."

"Which is a way of telling me there's no hope for the kid," I muttered.

"There comes a time, Al, when we have to stand by and watch someone die."

I paused at the door. "Nothing on earth could help him, I suppose."

"On earth?" He wagged his head. "Not that I know of."

From Martin's I went to see Allan Comer. We talked about little David's case, then I said, "Tell me, pastor, how far can we go with the thing we call faith?"

"How far? There's no limit, I suppose. The Bible says all things are possible to him that believes."

"Will you ask the church to pray for David?"

He nodded. "Sunday morning, Al."

That night I wrote my second story on David. I put in the words of my pastor. I reported that the church was going to pray for David.

The national press grabbed that story, too, and so did television. Letters poured in by the hundreds.

People everywhere, who believed in the power of prayer, were praying for David.

But when I went to see David again, I found his mother had suppressed the news in her home. David knew nothing about what was happening.

"You have no business doing a thing like that!" I cried. "Let the boy know that the people are praying for him. It will help his own faith."

"So he'll build up a false hope—then die! No! I can't endure this mockery! He's not your son. You don't know how I feel. I'm his mother!"

"I wish he were my kid!" I said softly. "I'd like to have a kid like that some day. How he ever got to be what he is, though, with a father and mother like he had is beyond me!"

Her eyes blazed. "His father and mother?"

"Yes."

"Please go. Go!"

I went out, and it was snowing pretty hard. I drove to my apartment, but I didn't go in. I began to walk. From far off I heard a voice singing, "Come, all ye faithful." I thought of little David, and the tears stung my eyes. I raised my face and felt the snow cold on it, and I breathed a prayer to the God who came to a cattle shed to save mankind, to come to a kid who had leukemia. And standing there in the snow, praying, suddenly I felt as if He was in the world in a special way, as He had been that first Christmas, and my heart trembled with a strange joy. I seemed to feel, too, the prayers of hundreds of people, all praying for little David

Stone. I had never felt so lifted in spirit before in my life.

They put me on a special assignment the next morning, and I had to leave Springfield. I returned a few days later to find the Old Man all excited.

"Al, you've really got a story now! I've been holding things back for you. It is your story, you know."

"What gives?"

"Mrs. Stone phoned an hour ago. She asked for you. She says David is well!"

"What?"

"Don't stand there and gape. Get out there, man!"

I grabbed a phone. When a voice answered I said, "Dr. Martin, this is Al. What about David Stone? Have you seen him?"

"Yes." There was a pause. "I'm the one who told Mrs. Stone that David is all right."

"What happened?"

"Mrs. Stone phoned me that David insisted on getting up, that he was well. She was wrought up, so I went out. He looked so good I took a blood specimen and checked again with Dr. Gaffel. The boy doesn't have leukemia!"

"But the diagnosis! You said it was certain."

"It was, Al. Believe me."

"Well, what do you say?"

"I'm a scientist, Al. I don't know for sure whether the medicine we've given him had anything to do with the boy's recovery or not. I don't even know if the recovery will last. If you ask me, frankly, I think all those prayers had something to do with it. Faith— who knows what it might accomplish?"

I found Carol Stone weeping, but she smiled at me radiantly. Suddenly David stood in the doorway in pajamas. He said, "Hi, Al! I feel fine. We're going to have a swell Christmas, aren't we, Mother?"

Carol ran and hugged him to her heart. "Oh, yes, darling! We're going to have a wonderful Christmas. Wonderful!"

"It's the day to remember God's birthday," said David.

I sat down on the davenport, and David came and sat down by me. He reached for my hand, then sat gazing happily at the Christmas tree.

"It's beautiful," he said, "like God."

Carol said, "I should know more about Him, shouldn't I?"

I put my arm about David's shoulders. "I think Dave and I might be fair teachers. If you're listening."

"I'm listening."

Later, as I drove back to the *Daily Eagle* through swirling snow, remembering the tender look on Carol's face and the new faith shining in her eyes, I knew this was going to be a very happy Christmas indeed.

The Why of Christmas

Don Dedera

There are stories . . . and there are stories. This is one of the latter. The writer, a good friend of mine, is today one of the most prolific freelance writers who cover the American Southwest. Before Dedera assumed the editorship of Arizona Highways, *for a number of years he wrote a column for* The Arizona Republic. *In order to come up with new material he became a voracious reader of small-town newspapers across the state. It was in one of these that he noticed an unusual thank you emanating out of the little town of Why. Intrigued, he called Peggy Kater, proprietor of the Why Trading Post, and asked for details. The resulting story was run in* The Arizona Republic *in December 1967.*

As I was speaking with Dedera recently—today he operates his own small publishing operation—about this Christmas collection, he observed that he knew of a Christmas story, one that he had chronicled himself, that I might be interested in. A Christmas story he had never been able to forget: so much so that in 1992 it will again see print, this time in the December Arizona Highways, *a quarter of a century after he first came across it. Needless to say, I asked him to send the story post-haste as I needed one more story to complete the collection—not just a story but the story. And he delivered.*

MID-DECEMBER'S raindrops drill down like chill needles on this night in the tiny southwestern Arizona town with the oddest of placenames: Why. Sleet drapes the eaves of the Why Trading Post and glazes the lonesome road forks.

Bob, the Indian clerk, stomps through the front door with a filled kerosene can. He grumps, "Last summer during the drought our cows died of thirst. Now the roads run rivers. Gettin' slick. Snow by morning." He glowers into the gloom engulfing an Indian reservation twice the size of Delaware.

"Then go home, Bob," says the trading post owner, Peggy Kater. "I'll close up." Bob nods gratefully. Through the sodden darkness he is glad to hurry to his family many miles away, deep within Papagoland.

Normally Mrs. Kater keeps late hours, because some of her customers must travel 50 miles to shop. But probably none will come this night. In such foul weather the Papago gods themselves hide within their underground maze. Now alone, Mrs. Kater takes up her cherished chore: stuffing hundreds of stockings with treats and toys for her annual Christmas party.

Abruptly, the driving downpour bursts through the doorway and deposits a Tohono O'odham (Papago) family, blinking against the electric light. The young mother slings an infant on her hip. Two small barefoot boys leave wet tracks across the wooden floor. They stare silently at the sweets. Peggy hands them a taste.

"Aren't you cold without shoes—did you leave them at home?" blurts Mrs. Kater. She should have known better. In the year of 1967, poverty and privation among the Papago are commonplace. Why was just a Y in the road when Peggy and her husband moved here 20 years earlier, and they have watched it grow with electricity and telephone and water system and post office and modern roadside facilities for tourists passing through to Mexico and California.

But into the 1960s not much yet has improved the lot of a tribe that early befriended the Spanish priests, Forty-niners, American soldiers, and pioneer immigrants who crossed their lands. In fact, their hospitality may have accounted for an irony: the Papago were the last large tribe to be granted a reservation by the Great White Father.

The Indian mother drops her head in shame. In the Papago language she explains that this year the Bean People have found no work on the parched reservation, and that she and her family had journeyed north in hopes of harvesting cotton fields. But then long spells of rain had delayed the picking. Now they are hitchhiking back to their clay-and-cactus house at Hotason Vo.

They have no money for shoes—"only for *necessities.*"

Mrs. Kater frowns at the thin frayed shirts, the patched denims. This will not do. Impulsively she pulls down two new outfits from her shelves. Flannel shirts. Levis. Wool socks. Quilted jackets. And shoes. Expensive water repellent horsehide ankle tops.

The boys tense under the white woman's touch, but they submit to her measuring for sizes. Shyly they rub the synthetic fur coat collars. Then they grin with gaping teeth, realizing the clothes truly are their own, and will not be taken back.

Peggy prattles on, to bridge the awkward moments. By a wall of horsecollars the Indian woman weeps into a cup of her hand. The O'odham are a proud people who have always taken care of their own, when they can. The lessons of the oft-harsh desert and the parables of the Old Ones encourage a culture of sharing. To give is humankind's noblest virtue.

"No charge for the clothes. Now what are the *necessities?*"

In the early days the Papago father with much ritual might have fetched salt from a slough of the Sea of Cortez, a hundred miles to the south. Now he orders a blue cylinder of *on* (salt). Twenty-five pounds *chewy* (flour). Four pounds *monjic* (lard). Can of *espowla* (baking soda). For the tortillas, a sack of *moo* (pinto beans). For the beans, a slab of *chewhook* (fat beef). A box of .22 caliber shells for hunting rabbits.

Each item is ordered and purchased separately, so the remaining money might be measured against priorities. Peggy Kater babbles on, the living newspaper of Why. Indian customers and white residents alike admire and respect this woman who brought in the first water well, established a senior citizen trailer park, and, to serve 200 square miles of thinly populated desert, obtained the post office named Why.

"Why 'Why'?" the postmaster in Washington had asked.

"Why not?" was Peggy's response, and her logic won the day.

Now Peggy's chatter turns to coming events. "Remember the Christmas party," she says. "The kids are invited." The weather may improve. So-and-so got married. What's-his-name is sick.

And Peggy idly adds, "I had hoped to pick some of those seeds that taste like nuts, that you find on top of the Big Ajo Mountains. But the storm came, and . . ."

Time to go. There is no word in the Papago tongue for thanks. The people say it with their eyes. Then the couple vanish into the blackness, their bundled-up boys bounding behind, like warm, wooly pups.

* * * * *

A week passes.

Under clearing skies preparations for the Fiesta of the Nativity are completed. Musicians and singers are on hand. Tubs of chili con carne bubble over coals. Fry bread sizzles in pots of tallow. Tamales steam inside their cornhusk wrappers. Hidden away is a Santa Claus suit, to appear when the towering stacks of mesquite feed the evening bonfires.

At sundown Quee-wich-choo (Under Tree) plays his ancient flute, and beats a deerhide drum. His brother dances—brass shells and bells at his belt, rattles from knee to ankle. As the traditional half-

Papago legend, half-Christian ceremony begins, two little Papagos dart across the clearing and stop in front of a white woman. All eyes turn to the two gap-toothed boys, shyly handing a basket to Mrs. Kater. Baskets are fairly common in Papago country—however, this one is anything but common-appearing. It is exquisite, lovingly fashioned from pastel yucca fibers.

Her efforts to thank them fail, however. They urge her to open it.

To humor them, and to enable the celebration to continue, she acquiesces, gently opening the delicate little basket.

She gasps in disbelief. . . . It *can't* be! . . . But it is: eight little seeds, seeds that taste like nuts, seeds that grow only on the top of the Big Ajo Mountains.

Whirling through her mind in milliseconds are images: early on a bitterly cold December morning, while it is yet dark, two little boys rising from their mats and stealthily slipping out of the mud-and-wattle hut so as not to wake the rest of the family. By the time daylight reveals the looming black heights of the Ajo Mountains they have put miles behind their feet.

They begin the long climb into the mists. There are no roads, scarcely any paths . . . as they zig-zag up the great wall of rock, fighting brush, cactus, and assorted spiny plants all the way. . . . A thousand feet above the plain below, they stop and look back at the long way they've come . . . Two thousand feet. . . . Three thousand feet. . . . The sun climbs and the unmarked way gets steeper and steeper. . . . Four thousand feet above the desert floor, and now they are forced to deal with snow and ice. Yet still they climb on.

Almost a mile above the only world they know they at last reach the perilous cliffs where struggle for existence a few scattered trees—stunted and battered by fierce winter storms and the sizzling furnace blasts of summer. Occasionally seeds, seeds good to eat, can be found in these trees—that is, if the mountain squirrels or birds don't get to them first.

Danger, danger all around. And one fall would be the last fall. . . . Yet the two boys skirt the abyss and dare their way to the eyries preferred by these most inhospitable trees. Somehow . . . they *must* find these seeds, these precious seeds that represent the only thank you in their power to give.

The shadows lengthen dangerously before they reluctantly give up the search and begin their long descent with all the treasure they can find: eight insignificant-looking little seeds. During the dangerous climb down they edge their way from tree to tree, from clump of brush to clump of brush, from outcropping to outcropping. Frequently, they stop and discuss how to traverse the late afternoon iced-over streams.

At long last, when they feel they can't possibly endure the vertical descent any longer, the shadowed land finally begins to slope more gently . . . and far below, in the setting sun, they see the wattled walls of home.

It is night when they wearily step into the hut. Mutely they open their hands and reveal the eight seed nuts. . . . They are afraid. . . . Was it wrong to risk their lives just to find eight little seeds? Eight seeds for a white lady who may not even value them at all. Father looks across the fire at Mother. Neither speaks for some time. Finally, Father gets up, walks to the doorway, and peers into the night; peers northeast toward Baboquivari Peak, in ancient times the seat of Eé-e-toy, the Great Spirit. Meanwhile, the boys and their mother wait silently for the verdict.

At last, Father steps back inside, with an air of resolution. He turns to the boys and declares, "It is well. . . . Eé-e-toy would be pleased—the Tohono O'odham pay their debts."

The decision made, the boys turn naturally to Mother for implementation. "We must find a basket to put them in," she declares, "not just any basket . . . but a basket worthy of the gift." Her head in hand, she ponders a while, then straightens, having found the answer: "Tomorrow, go down to the big rock that shelters the clump of 'ee-hooks'—the white man calls them 'devil's claw,' and bring me back the seed pods. I shall combine them with that yucca fiber I have been saving for a very special basket."

* * * * *

The two boys stand there . . . still . . . and they wonder why it is that the white lady is so silent. . . . Is she unhappy with them because they were able to find only eight seeds? . . . Why doesn't she thank them in the usual way of white folks: many words spoken quickly?

But then . . . they look up to the quivering lips and beyond: they understand as they see the tears.

Bethany's Christmas Carol

Mabel McKee

This story has long been one of my family's favorites. It depicts how little it avails if one has wealth without personal caring. Also, that much "illness" is in reality the result of wounds to the spirit. Equally important, it exemplifies how important it is that nurses genuinely care for and love their patients.

THEY called her Carol Meloney 11 months of the year at Bethany Hospital. But during the twelfth, which was December, they termed her "Christmas Carol," and she was so merry and happy that most of the patients there thought that was the sole reason the dusky-eyed, auburn-haired little nurse was called a Christmas name.

But the head of the nurses and all the others down to the newest probationer could have told you that the reason was because Carol was born on Christmas Day just 21 years before! Also that her frail little mother, who had seen five little brothers and sisters come into the parsonage home before Carol, declared that her newest baby sang instead of cried on that Christmas Day she was born, and had said to her minister husband, "Let's call her Carol, dear."

Always in that parsonage home, from which the mother soon slipped away, they called her "Carol, dear," and she was as fragrant and sweet and lovely as a Christmas Carol.

But this Christmas week, Carol wasn't happy; didn't want to sing. Down in the baby ward lay her wee namesake, until a week ago snuggled beside its little mother. But that little mother had, without warning, slipped away, leaving her precious baby to the happy nurse of Bethany whose name she had given it because she wanted the baby to be merry and cheerful and lovable, too—had slipped away without breaking her silence or letting anybody there know who were her relatives, if she had any, or if there were some other persons with a claim on the child.

Carol lifted the little one in her arms and said, "I'm going to keep her in my own family. The mother really gave her to me, you know. There is my oldest sister, Marie, both of whose babies died a year ago. I'm going to ask Marie to keep her because she is another Christmas Carol."

Standing there close beside the tiny basket bed, Carol had made all her plans. She would go home to

Marie on Christmas Day, and she would lay the baby in her arms and say, "I've brought you another Christmas Carol, dear, whose mother has slipped away just as mine did while I was still a babe."

Marie *couldn't* refuse to keep the baby, and the child would take the lonely ache out of Marie's heart. Oh, this Christmas promised to be the very happiest one she had known, just because she had such a wonderful gift to give. But "best-laid schemes o' mice and men gang aft a-gley." Young Dr. Greig assigned her to the peritonitis case in Room 26 when the regular nurse came down with the measles. The patient refused to change nurses again, and since she was really quite ill, no one dared offend her.

Carol looked down at the white toes of her Oxfords when the superintendent told her that she would have to change her plans about going home for Christmas, and then the tears came in spite of her best efforts.

"Oh, I'm not thinking of myself," the girl sobbed, "but if Marie doesn't get my blessed baby as a Christmas present, I'm afraid she'll not have such a happy holiday."

The head nurse patted Carol's red-brown curls. "Patient in 26 is sick at heart as well as in body," she confided. "We assigned you to the case because we thought that you could cheer her up. She and her husband have been drawing apart for a long time. She is grieving, and it's your duty to try to coax bitterness from her heart and smiles back to her lips."

Carol found Mrs. Joseph Cartwright an ideal patient, in spite of what people said about her being a bit queer. When her friends sent her great boxes of flowers, she always divided them with some patients who had none. She introduced the young nurse to the club women who came to see her, and in every way treated her with such consideration that at times she felt like a sister to the rich woman.

But when everybody was gone, Mrs. Cartwright just turned her face toward the wall and lay very still, speaking to Carol only when she wanted something. She even protested when the girl brought in two holly wreaths for the windows. "I do not celebrate Christmas anymore, my dear," she explained. "Take the wreaths to someone who can share the Christmas spirit."

On this morning before Christmas Day she seemed more nervous than usual, and the doctor took Carol outside of the room. "Don't let her have visitors today," he warned. "They will only make her remember other holidays which have been happier. We must keep her from doing much of that, or she will have a relapse."

Carol was almost ready to go shopping then. Her eyes held a glint of happy anticipation. All her presents for her own people had been sent home, but she had to get an array of gifts for tiny Carol. The other nurses at Bethany wanted to help make the orphan baby's first Christmas a special one.

She found the best substitute in the hospital for

her patient, and then started on her way upstairs, to her own room. She heard the choir next door practicing Christmas carols. They would sing them that evening in the hospital, winding through the corridors and stopping at the doors of patients who were convalescing.

Carol listened. "Away in a manger," they began, and immediately she thought of the tiny baby which was now hers, lying in its plain little basket in the baby ward, and though she had a dozen things to do, the girl ran through the garlanded halls, down the stairs to the floor below, and into the baby's room, where she lifted her wee namesake and held her close in her arms.

"Marie's darling baby!" she whispered. "You're going to make our Marie happy again and drive away the sad shadows from her eyes. You little precious!"

The tiny baby was beautiful, with tiny petal-like hands, cupid's bow mouth, and hair that was going to be golden. She was dressed in a little white slip of the regulation hospital style. Carol was to get her a beautiful nainsook dress, delicately embroidered, with the money the other nurses had given. Oh, how hard it was for her to wait until she could get to town and select it!

Back into the gay corridors she skipped, and down the stairs just in time to meet a messenger boy with a package for her patient. It bore the seal of the city's most expensive jewelry shop. When the boy seemed bewildered, Carol offered to take it to Mrs. Cartwright.

Perhaps that is all she would have known about the jeweler's box had not the substitute asked her to stay a moment while she made a telephone call, and Carol stayed, straightening a magazine here or a bottle there as she waited.

The gleam of platinum caught her attention. The package had been unwrapped and disclosed a beautiful white satin box in which was an expensive wrist watch, a wreath with diamonds surrounding the face. Mrs. Cartwright's hand held the white card on which were the words, "Christmas Greetings," and the gray one under it which bore, in engraved letters, "Joseph Cartwright."

One long minute she studied the cards and the gift, then snapped the white velvet box shut and laid it on the table beside her bed. Tears trickled from between her closed eyelids.

Carol had seen it all through the big mirror, even the two cards which carried no hint of the affection that changes gifts from cold, inanimate things to love tokens.

"Oh, the poor dear!" she sighed, "why couldn't he have just said, 'with love'?"

The substitute nurse came back, and Carol hurried out into the spicy cold—hurried by all the late shoppers with their odd-shaped parcels, passed people who smiled and called "Merry Christmas" to each other through the falling snow, and as she hurried she sang softly to herself.

At the corner she decided to carry a great bowl of holly into Mrs. Cartwright's room that evening. At the next one she decided to carry tiny Carol into that room the next morning and see if the little Christmas visitor couldn't change that tired, heartbroken look into a tender smile. At the third corner she decided to buy Mrs. Cartwright a gift and write on the card, "With love—Carol."

At the big store where she bought tiny Carol's Christmas dress, little wool shirts and stockings, and a pink-and-white wooly baby blanket, she went on the quest for a gift for the sick lady. She didn't have much to spend. All the brothers and sisters and nieces and nephews had sadly depleted her purse. And wee Carol had almost finished it. She never dreamed that babies were such expensive bits of joy.

She wandered to the book counter. She thought of a gift book, full of sentiment, and with a beautiful binding. The head of the department came to wait on her. Carol liked the "head" for she loved books as she did people, and talked of them as if they were alive.

"I'm buying a little book for Mrs. Joseph Cartwright," she confided. "Do you know her?"

"Know her? I should say I do. Why, she used to bring her little son in here for me to help her choose his nursery rhyme books. She was the most adorable mother I ever knew."

"Oh," Carol's eyes opened wide. "I didn't know she had a little boy. She never mentions him. She's ill at Bethany Hospital, and I am her nurse."

The other woman's hands clasped Carol's. "Didn't you know she had a little boy? He died about three years ago! Haven't you ever heard what a bitter tragedy her home life has become?"

Then Carol felt more than pity for her patient—felt understanding and real love. Meanwhile the girl was talking—telling of Mrs. Cartwright's generous gifts to orphanages, to charity institutions, to every place that held a needy child.

Swayed by a new feeling, Carol bought the most beautiful book in the department and a dainty Christmas card, which read:

"I'm giving myself instead of wealth,
    And all I have to you."

She knew, somehow, that Mrs. Cartwright would really know she meant it. Hugging the bundles in her arms, she went out into the snow, to be pelted on the way home by two little boys with snowballs, to race down the avenue with other belated Christmas shoppers, and tell everybody who passed her, "Merry Christmas."

She had forgotten the disappointment she had felt because she couldn't be with her family. She was thinking of Christmas now as a day to especially love and be especially interested in the whole wide, weary world.

As she passed the tiny chapel on the corner, she slipped in to see the beautiful decorations. Just above the chancel hung a painting of the Christ as a tiny babe in the rude Bethlehem manger, and underneath it was the inscription:

"He gave the world's greatest Gift to all."

It was right then the beautiful Christmas idea was

born in her heart. It came with a cruel twist, though it was beautiful. She *couldn't* do it, she told herself. She would be robbing not only herself, but Marie, whom she loved so dearly. For she knew the little baby would bring joy to Marie through all the years that followed.

"But Marie can love another baby," the voice said. "Hasn't she often talked of adopting one? All you need to do is to encourage her, and she'll go right to an orphanage and get one."

Carol clasped her hands in front of her and knelt and prayed. Was it right for her to give away this baby, to whom the mother had given her name? Would it bring joy to Mrs. Cartwright's heart? Would she accept the gift, even if it were offered?

"You can offer it," the voice whispered. "You can *try* to bring her great joy." Carol bowed her head still lower. Lovingly she held close to her heart the miniature nainsook dress she had bought for her tiny namesake. And as she held it, there came to her mind the message her mother had left for her when she slipped away a few weeks after her birth: "I'm giving you to your sisters, dear baby, so they will not miss me so much. Babies heal heartaches better than anything else can. You were my Christmas gift, so I know you will be a love baby and love girl and then a love woman, who will love others all through your life."

Marie had told her that many, many times when she had been naughty and selfish in her childhood— told her that she must never cause anything except happiness, because she was a Christmas Carol to sing through the years.

Carol held the tiny dress closer and looked at the picture. "I'll give it for Your sake, Jesus." Back in her room again she unpacked the little bundles, laid the nainsook dress and Christmas card close together, then slipped up to Mrs. Cartwright's room. The patient had had her supper, the substitute said, and did not wish to be disturbed.

Carol went to the baby ward next, took tiny Carol back to her room, dressed her in the nainsook dress, and wrapped her in the pink-and-white blanket. Then she carried her to Mrs. Cartwright's room, entered softly on tiptoe, laid the tiny mite in the curve of her patient's arm, put the card in her hand, then slipped out before the sick woman could turn her head.

Carol's bell rang sharply half an hour later. Breathlessly she answered the call. Mrs. Cartwright's curved arm still held the baby. Her mouth was smiling though her eyes were misty.

"Oh, my dear, my dear," she began, "how could you be so generous as to give the tiny Christmas Carol you had planned to take to your sister? Oh, the wonder of your gift!" (The substitute only that afternoon had told Mrs. Cartwright the story of the tiny baby which Carol loved so dearly.) She was going to keep the baby. She wanted to adopt it, and wished a message sent asking Mr. Cartwright to come at once.

"He always wanted me to take a baby into our home," she whispered to Carol, "but until you gave me little Carol, I felt I couldn't hold one in my arms after Billy died."

Half an hour later Carol heard a rush outside the door and saw a big man, whom she instantly knew as Mr. Cartwright, coming into the room. This time she fairly ran out into the hall, where she felt herself the most lonely person in the whole world. She wandered on until she reached the corridor where the choir from the near-by church and nurses off duty were forming in line, ready for their march through the hospital. She heard the "specials" gently opening doors so their patients would not miss the singing.

She slipped into the line, right after the probationer whose mother had died a few weeks before, and patted the girl's shoulder comfortingly and held her hand as they began to march. Her other hand held one of the open song books, and her sweet, girlish soprano sang with the others.

They passed the men's ward and the old veteran, whose Grand Army button shone as did his eyes, waved his hand at them; passed the women's ward where there was a little lame girl keeping time to the music with her crutch; passed many other rooms, and entered the corridor off of which opened the room Carol had just left.

She glanced through the door ajar. Mrs. Cartwright still held the baby close to her heart, and her hand was resting on the bowed head of her husband. Her eyes were so beautiful and brilliant that Carol knew the spirit of Christmas was in her heart at last.

94

A Few Bars in the Key of G

Author Unknown

Probably my favorite of all Christmas stories set in the Old West is this one. You are carried along pell mell with the racing tide of the O'Henry-ish narrative, not knowing till the conclusion what in the world is really going on.

IT WAS 2:00 and time for the third watch on the night herd. There, two facts gradually impressed themselves on the consciousness of John Talbot Waring, as he was thumped into wakefulness by the Mexican "house-wrangler."

He unrolled his slicker, which had been serving as a pillow, enveloped himself in its clammy folds, and went out into the drizzling rain.

The cattle were unusually quiet, needing little attention, and Waring had ample opportunity to reflect on the disadvantages of a cow-puncher's life, as he rode slowly along the edge of the black mass of sleeping animals. The rain dripped from the limp brim of his sombrero; the chill wind, sweeping down from the mountains, pierced his damp clothes and made him shiver in the saddle. For the hundredth time within a week, Waring condemned himself for relinquishing the comforts of civilization for this hard life of Colorado.

He recalled his arrival on the range, six months before, a tenderfoot, and the various tribulations he had endured incident to his transformation into a full-fledged cowpuncher.

Of the hardships and dangers that come to every rider of the range, he had experienced his share, and faced them bravely, thereby winning the respect of the rough, lion-hearted men among whom he had cast his lot.

But all the weary months had been wasted; he had failed his object—he could not forget. It even seemed to him that instead of growing more endurable with time, the soreness in his heart and the sting of regret increased with every day. He wondered if she felt the separation; if she cared. As his thoughts wandered back over the past two years, he recalled every incident of their acquaintance. The day he had first seen her, as she stepped gracefully out beside the piano to sing—the song she had sung:

"The hours I spent with thee, dear heart,
Are as a string of pearls to me."

Then the sweet days which followed—their enjoyment together of symphony, oratorio, and opera.

He could see her as she appeared on that wonderful day when he had met her at the altar of the church, and spoken the words that were to bring them together through life. How beautiful she was, and how proud he had been of her as they walked down the broad aisle.

He looked back at their wedding trip as a beautiful dream. How well he remembered the return to the lovely home he had prepared for her, and the first dear days within the walls. How happy they had been, and how he had loved her; *had* loved her? He *did* love her.

And then the shadow had come over their home. He asked himself bitterly why he had not been more patient with her, and made allowances for her high spirits or moods in their quarrels. She was such a child. He could see now that he had been wrong. Never! The words she had spoken in the heat of her anger had burned themselves into his heart. He also recalled every word of his response:

"Your words convince me that we cannot live together any longer. I will neither forget nor forgive them. I am going away."

That was all. Without another word he had left her, standing white and motionless in the center of her dainty chamber, and gone from the beautiful home to come out here to the wildest spot he could find, and plunge into the perilous life he was now leading, in the vain effort to forget.

Then his thoughts strayed to the strange postal card he had received the day before. It had been directed in care of his attorney and forwarded by his lawyer to the remote mountain post-office where Waring received his mail. It was an ordinary postal card, its peculiarity consisting in the fact that the communication on the back was composed, not in words, but in music—four measures in the key of G. He had hummed the notes over and over, and thought they had a strangely familiar sound, yet he could not place the fragment, nor even determine the composer. It had a meaning, of that he was convinced, but what could it be? Who could have sent it? Among his friends were many musicians, any one of whom might have adopted such a method of communication with him. He began to hum the phrase as he rode around the cattle.

Suddenly, while in the midst of a passage from one of the great works of a master composer, he stopped short in surprise. He was singing the notes on the card. It had come to him like a flash. He wrote some words beneath the notes. There was no mistake. He had solved the mystery.

Pulling up with a jerk that almost lifted the iron-jawed bronco from the ground, he hurled himself from the saddle and reached the "Boss" in two bounds.

"I must be in Denver tonight! I want your best horse quick! It's only 60 miles to Empire, and I can get the train there. It leaves at 1:00, and I can make it, if you'll lend me Star. I know he's your pet horse, but I tell you, Mr. Coberly, this means everything to me. I simply must get there. I tell you—"

"You ought to know, Jack, that I won't lend Star;

so what's the use of askin'? What's the matter with you that you're in such a confounded rush?"

Waring drew the "Boss" beyond earshot of the listening cowpunchers, spoke to him rapidly and earnestly, finally handing him the postal card, which Coberly scanned intently. A change came over his face.

"Why didn't you show me this card at first? Of course you can have the horse. Hi, there; some of you boys round up the horses and rope Star for Mr. Waring."

In an incredibly short time, a rush of hoofs announced the arrival of the horses. A dozen hands made quick work of saddling, and with a hurried goodby all around, Waring swung himself up and astride the magnificent animal and was off on his long ride.

The long pacing strides of Coberly's pet covered the ground in a surprising manner and 8:00 found 20 miles behind his nimble feet. A five-minute stop, and then on across country to the stage station, 15 miles away. It lacked 20 minutes of 10:00 when Waring drew rein. He unsaddled and turned the big thoroughbred into the corral. A half hour's rest would put new life into him. Twenty-two miles to the railroad, and nearly three hours in which to cover it. But the range must be crossed and Waring knew that the next 10 miles of steep climbing to the summit of Berthoud Pass meant more than twice that distance on the flat plain.

At 10:15, Star was carrying him up the road. Up and up they went, mile after mile. Two miles from the top, Waring dismounted and led his panting horse along the icy trail. The rare air seemed to burn his lungs as he struggled up the remaining distance to the summit of the pass, 12,000 feet above the sea.

Down at last to the level road they came, with five miles still to go. Rounding a turn in the road he spied a horseman approaching. The stranger eyed him sharply as he drew near, and suddenly whipped out a six-shooter.

"Hold up, there. I want to know where you are going with Joe Coberly's horse."

"I've been working for Coberly, and he lent me the horse to ride over here to catch the next train."

"That yarn won't do. I know old Joe, and I happen to know that he wouldn't a lent that horse to his own brother, let alone one of his cowpunchers,. I guess I'll have to lock you up till the boys come over after you."

"Look here, Mr. Sheriff, I'm telling you the truth."

"It's no use, my friend; your story won't hold water. Why're you in such a tearin' hurry, anyway?"

Waring remembered the postal card. He reached into his breast pocket and produced it. "That's my reason for haste," he said, "and that is why Coberly let me take his horse," and he added a few words of explanation.

Keeping the captive covered with the muzzle of his gun, the officer took the card. As he read it, his face lighted up and his revolver lowered.

"That's all right, youngster. I'm sorry I stopped

you. I hope you won't miss the train. I'll ride down to the station with you, as some of the boys might want to string you up on account of the horse—everybody knows him."

In a few moments they saw the town before them a mile distant. The train was at the station. A touch of the spur, and Star stretched out into a run that left the sheriff behind. The black smoke began to come in heavy puffs from the funnel of the engine, and the line of cars moved slowly away from the station. Then it was that Star showed the spirit he was made of. He bounded forward and swept down upon the town like a whirlwind.

As the crowd of train-time loafers lounged around the station, their attention was attracted to the two swiftly approaching riders, and they paused to watch the race. Presently one cried:

"Hello, that first horse is Coberly's black, and he's sure movin' too. The other fellow ain't in it. Why, it's the sheriff and he's after the other chap. Horse thief!"

The others took up the cry of "Horse thief!" and as Waring flashed past the building at Star's top speed, a volley of shots greeted him. Fortunately they went wild, and before any more could be fired, the sheriff tore into the crowd and roared, "Stop shooting. That man's all right. He's only trying to catch the train." Then there was a mad rush to the track, where a view of the race could be obtained.

Waring, with eyes fixed and jaws set, was riding desperately. Thirty feet—the spectators in the door-way of the last car gazed breathlessly. Twenty feet—and still he gained. Only five feet now! Inch by inch he crawled up. He was abreast of the platform! Swerving his flying horse close to the track, Waring leaned over, and grasping the railing with both hands, lifted himself free from the saddle, shook his feet from the stirrups, and swung himself over the steps of the car. The faint sound of a cheer reached him from the distant depot.

As the train neared Denver, Waring remembered something he had forgotten in his excitement; that the banks would probably be closed and that he would probably be unable to cash a check. But the postal card had served well thus far; perhaps its mission was not ended.

Jumping into a carriage, he was driven to the nearest drugstore where he consulted a directory.

"To 900 South Seventeenth Street," he cried, as he entered the vehicle. Arriving at his destination, he sprang out and, saying "Wait," ran up the steps of the palatial residence.

To the dignified butler who opened the door, he said, "I wish to see Mr. Foster. My name is Waring. I haven't a card with me."

That gentleman entered immediately.

"Mr. Foster, you are the president of the Denver National Bank, which I believe handles the Western interests of the Second National Bank of Boston?"

"Yes."

"I have an account at the Second, and I want you to cash a check for me. It is after banking hours, I

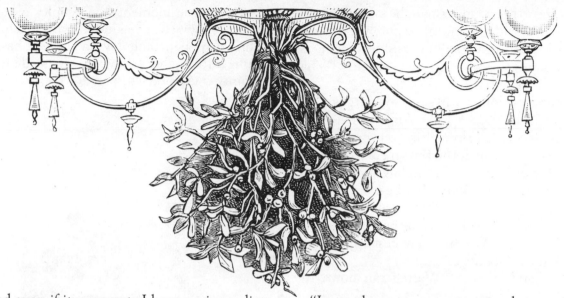

know, and even if it were not, I have no immediate means of identification. It is of the greatest importance that I take the Eastern express tonight, or I would not come to you in this irregular way—"

"One moment, Mr. Waring. Pardon me for interrupting you but it will save your time as well as my own if I say that what you ask is impossible, as you should know. My advice is that you wire your bank for money."

"Of course, I know I can do that, but it means a day's delay, and that is what I want to avoid. See here, Mr. Foster, I am willing to apply any amount within reason, for this accommodation, if you will oblige me."

"It must be a very urgent matter that requires such haste. Really, Mr. Waring, I must positively decline to do anything for you."

"It is an urgent matter," and he told of the postal card and its purpose, adding a brief account of his efforts to get into the city in time to take the train that night.

"Let me see the card. From what is it taken, did you say?"

Upon hearing the answer, he left the room to return in a few moments with a musical score, which he had laid upon the table, and turned the pages until he found what he sought. Carefully he compared the music on the card with that on the printed sheet.

Then, turning to the younger man, he said, "I will see to this myself; it will, of course, be purely a personal matter, as it is contrary to all my business methods, but I cannot resist such an appeal as this. What amount do you require?"

"One hundred dollars will serve my purpose."

"Make your check for 150. You will need that much unless you care to travel in your present costume. You can cash this at the Brown Palace Hotel. I will phone the cashier, so you will have no trouble."

Waring tried to thank him but he would not listen.

"You are perfectly welcome, my boy. I am glad to be able to help you. You have my best wishes for a pleasant journey. Goodbye."

A swift handclasp and Waring ran down the steps.

"Telegraph office," he shouted. Then, minutes later, these words were speeding over the wire:

"Postal received. Arrive Boston, Friday night. See Luke 1:13—Jack."

When the Chicago Limited pulled out of Denver that evening, John Talbot Waring, attired in the garments of the most approved fashion, was standing on the rear platform of the Pullman, softly humming from the great oratorio, "The Messiah." There was a tender light in his eyes as he gazed at the postal card he held in his hand. And these were the words he read:

"For unto us a child is born;
Unto us a son is given."

At the same moment 2,000 miles away in the East, a pale young wife was holding a telegram close to her lips. An open Bible lay on the bed beside her. Turning softly on her pillow, she glanced lovingly at the dainty cradle and whispered, "Thou shalt call his name John."

Why the Minister Did Not Resign

Author Unknown

One of the first Christmas stories I can remember my mother reciting—many were by memory—is this one. My mother puts all of herself into her recitations: laughing in hilarious passages and crying in moving ones. This is one of her tear-jerkers; to the best of my knowledge she never got through this Hatfield-McCoyish tale dry-eyed. Neither did her audiences.

H E WAITED until she put the baby down, then he met her in the middle of the room and said it.

"I shall do it next Sabbath, Rebekah."

"O Julius, not *next* Sabbath!" she cried out in dismay. "Why, next Sabbath is Christmas, Julius!"

Julius Taft's smooth-shaven lips curled into a smile.

"Well, why not, little woman? It would be a new way to celebrate Christmas. Everyone likes a 'new way.' The holly and the carols are so old!"

"Julius!"

"Forgive me, dear; but my heart is bitter. I cannot bear it any longer. I shall do it next week, Rebekah."

"But afterward, Julius?"

The mother's eyes wandered to the row of little chairs against the wall, each with its neatly folded little clothes. There were three little chairs and the baby's crib. Afterward, what about those? They argued mutely against this thing.

"Afterward, I'll dig ditches to earn bread for the babies—don't worry, little mother!" he laughed unsteadily. Then he drew her down with him on the sofa.

"Let's have it out, dear. I've borne it alone as long as I can."

"Alone!" she scolded softly. "Julius Taft, you know I've been bearing it with you!"

"I know it, dear; but we've both kept still. Now let's talk it out. It's no use beating about the bush, Rebekah, I've got it to do."

"O Julius, if we could only peacemake!" she wailed.

"But we can't—not even the minister's little peacemaker wife. They won't let us do it—they'd rather wrangle."

She put her hand across his lips to stifle the ugly word; but she knew it applied.

"They don't realize, Julius. If Mrs. Cain and Mrs.

Drinkwater would only realize! They influence all the rest. Everyone would make up, if they would. They're the ones to peacemake, Julius."

"Yes, but Drinkwaters and Cains won't 'peacemake'—you can't make oil and water unite. There was a grudge between them three generations ago, and it's descending. I can't see any way out of it."

"But on Christmas, Julius! 'Peace on earth, good will to men,' " Rebekah Taft murmured softly. The minister sighed heavily.

"There isn't any 'peace, good will' in the Saxon church, Rebekah. It won't be any special service. It will be just like all the other services, only the minister will resign."

"But he will preach a Christmas sermon, Julius? Tell me he will!" pleaded the minister's little peacemaker wife.

"Yes, dear, he will preach a Christmas sermon to please his little wife."

They sat quite silent awhile. The sleeping baby nestled and threw out a small pink-and-white hand aimlessly. The clock on the painted mantel said, "Bedtime, bedtime, bedtime!" with monotonous repetition.

They were both very tired, but they still sat side by side on the hard little sofa, thinking the same sorrowful thoughts. It was the wife who first broke the silence.

"Dear, there are so many things to think about," she whispered.

He smiled down at her from his superior height.

"Four things," he counted on his fingers. "Katie, Julius Junior, Hop-o'-My-Thumb, and the baby!"

"Yes, I meant the children. If you—"

Julius Taft was big and broad-shouldered. He drew himself up and faced her. His lean, good face was the face of a man who would create the opportunity that he could not find ready to his hand.

"Did the children's mother think all I could do was to preach?" he cried gaily. He could not bear the worry in her dear face. "She's forgotten I blew the bellows in my father's smithy. I can blow them again! I can find good, honest work in God's world, dear heart, never fear, and it will be infinitely better than preaching to a divided people."

"Yes, it will be better," she agreed; and then they listened to the clock.

The little church at Saxon had its feud. It had brought it a certain kind of fame in all the countryside. Other churches pointed to it with indulgent pity. Strangers over in Krell and Dennistown were regaled with entertaining accounts of how the Saxon congregation was divided by the broad aisle into two hostile factions, and no man stepped across.

"It's the dead line," chuckled the Krell newsmonger-in-chief. "No one but the minister dares go across! Those for the Cain side sit on one side of the aisle, and those for the Drinkwater side sit on the other. The gallery is reserved for neutrals, but it's always empty! They make it terrible hard for their parson over there in Saxon."

The Krell newspaper was right. It was terribly hard for the minister at Saxon. For eight years he and his gentle little wife had struggled to calm the troubled waters, but still they flowed on turbulently. Still there was discord, whichever way one turned. Another congregation might have separated farther than a broad aisle's width long ago, and worshiped in two churches instead of one. But the Saxon congregation had its own way of doing things. Its founders had been original, and generation upon generation had inherited the trait.

Midway in the week preceding Christmas, Julius Taft came to the little parsonage nursery, with signals of fresh distress plainly hoisted.

"Well?"

Rebekah Taft stopped rocking and waited. The baby in her arms lurched joyously toward the tall figure.

"Well, Julius?"

"Please, ma'am, may I come in and grumble, ma'am? I'm 'that' full I can't hold in! Here, give me the youngster. What do you suppose has happened now, little woman?"

"The church has blown up!" Rebekah responded.

"Not yet, but the fuse is lighted. I've just found out about the Christmas music. I hoped they would not have any."

"Oh, Julius, so did I! It will be sure to make trouble."

"It's made it already. That's it! I've just found out that Mrs. Cane is drilling her little Lethia to sing a carol; you know she has a beautiful little voice."

"Yes, oh, yes, as clear as a bird's. Why won't it be beautiful to have her sing, Julius?"

"Because Mrs. Drinkwater is drilling Gerry to sing," the minister said dryly.

"Oh!"

"And it won't be a duet, little woman."

They both laughed, and the shrill crow of the baby chimed in. Only the baby's laugh was mirthful. The minister's worn face sobered quickly.

"I don't know how it will come out," he sighed. "They are both very determined, and the hostile feeling is so strong. I wish it might have held off a little longer—till you and I got back to the smithy, dear!"

Out in the leafless orchard, back of the parsonage, a little group of children was collected together on a mild late December afternoon. The two factions that pertained among their elders was distinctly visible there. Two well-defined groups stood aloof, eyeing each other with family scorn. Between the two groups, midway, the minister's two little children stood, apparently in a conciliatory mood.

"Let's play meeting," suggested Julius Junior, the paternal mantle on his small, square shoulders. "I'll preach."

"Oh, yes, do let's!—we're so sick of playing battle," urged Kathie, eagerly. Battle was the favorite play, presumably on account of the excellent opportunities it offered the opposing parties.

"Sit down by the big log—there's a good place. This rock's my pulpit," bustled the little minister importantly, and the children scurried into place. It was noteworthy that the broad trunk of the old fallen tree set apart the rival factions. On each side squatted the divided congregation. Julius Junior's little lean brown face assumed a serious expression. He stood awhile in deep thought. Then his face brightened.

"I know! I'll preach you a Christmas sermon!" he cried softly. "That will be very ap-pro-perate, because Sabbath is Christmas, you know. Now, I'll begin. My text today is—is—I know! 'Peace on earth, good will to men,'—that's it—'Peace on earth, good will to men.'"

It was sunny and still in the orchard behind the parsonage. The rows of children's faces put on piety as a garment, and were staidly solemn. The small minister's face was rapt. Suddenly a high, sweet voice interrupted.

"I'll sing the carols," it cried.

"No, *I'll* sing 'em!"

"My mother's taught me how. I guess I'm the one that's going to sing 'em on Christmas!"

"I guess you aren't, Lethia Cain! I guess my mother's been teaching me."

"My mother says I'm going to sing 'em—so there, Gerry Drinkwater!"

"My mother says *I'm* going to—so there!"

The small rivals glared at each other. A murmur of supporting wrath rose behind each. The little minister looked worried—the paternal mantle weighed heavily.

"Hush!" he cried, earnestly. "We'll have congregational singing instead. Sit right down—I'm goin' to preach."

For a little there was only the sound of his earnest voice in the snowy orchard, with the soft, sighing wind for its only accompaniment. He preached with deep fervor. Two tiny spots of color blossomed out in his cheeks as he went on.

" 'Peace on earth,'—that means everybody's to be friends with everybody else," he said. "Everybody's to be peaceful an' loving, an' kind, same's the Lord Jesus was. Do you s'pose He'd have sat on the same side of the broad aisle every single Sabbath that ever was? No, my friends, I'll tell you what the Lord would have done. He'd have sat on your side up to the sermon, Lethia, and then He'd have gone 'cross, tiptoe an' soft, in His beautiful white robe, an' sat on Gerry's side clear through to the benediction—just to make 'peace on earth.' Can't you most see Him sitting there—"

The minister's little brown face shone with a solemn light.

"Can't you see how peaceful He'd have looked, an' how lovin'-kind? An' then my father'd have asked Him to say the benediction, an' He'd have spread out His hands over us an' said, softly, 'Peace on earth, good will to men,' an' that would have meant for us to love each other, an' sit together, and sing out o' the same hymnbook."

It was quiet under the leafless apple trees. All the

little faces were solemn. It was as if the white-robed Guest were among them, stepping across the dividing line, "tiptoe an' soft"—as if His hands were spread out over them in benediction.

"Peace on earth, good will to men."

The small faces gazed at each other solemnly. The minister went on with stanch courage, his hands unconsciously extended.

"It would have meant to sing your Christmas carols out o' the same hymnbook. Why don't you do it today, just as if He was here?"

He waited confidently, and not in vain. Two little figures, one at each end of the long log, stood up and began to sing. Gradually they drifted nearer until they stood side by side. Their high, childish voices blended sweetly.

* * * * *

Julius Taft worked on his Christmas sermon with a heavy heart. The war clouds seemed gathering ominously. Rumors of war crept in to him, in his quiet study.

"I don't know how it's coming out, little woman," he sighed. "I have done everything I can—I've been to see them both, those women. Both of them have their plans made unchangeably, and, if they collide, then—the crash."

"Yes, then the crash," sighed the minister's wife.

"I tried to persuade them both; you don't know how hard I worked, dear! But all the while I knew I was wasting time and would better come home to my sermon. Now I am going to wait; but, remember, something will happen tomorrow. Rebekah—two things."

"Two, Julius?"

"Yes; the minister's resignation and the crash."

He laughed, but his pale face smote her, and she crept on to his knee, and laid her own pale face against his. Somewhere in the house they could hear children's happy voices. It helped them.

"They are dear children, Julius," the mother whispered.

"God bless them!" he said.

"Yes—oh, yes, God bless them! And He will, Julius. I think our boy will be a preacher."

"Then the Lord help him," the minister cried.

* * * * *

Christmas morning dawned clear, crisp, and beautiful. Chimes in the bell tower tolled out their Christmas music, but the little carolers at Saxon were missing when church time came. Their mothers searched for them vainly. But both children had disappeared at the close of Sabbath school. No one could find them.

The last bell rang, and in despair, each mother gave up the search, and went to her seat alone. They were both fretted and disappointed, but were palpably relieved to discover that their losses were mutual.

In the minister's pew the minister's wife sat among her little brood with gentle dignity.

Service began and went on a little monotonously.

On both sides of the broad aisle there was evident keen disappointment, as though some anticipated relish had failed. Everyone had expected that something would happen. The absence of little Lethia Cain and Gerry Drinkwater dispelled the possibility.

The minister prayed in his earnest, direct way, and the opening hymn was announced. It was then that the something happened, after all. Suddenly, high, sweet music sounded in the people's ears—clear, high music, such as only the voices of little children can make. It came nearer—up the broad aisle! There were two voices. Two little children trudged up the aisle, hand in hand, singing a Christmas carol.

"Al-le-lu-ia! Al-le-lu-ia! Peace, good will—on—earth," the childish voices sang. They filled the quiet church with clear melody. The people's listening faces softened and grew gentle. The two mothers leaned forward, breathlessly.

"Al-le-lu-ia! Al-le-lu-ia!" high and sweet, triumphant. "Peace on earth, good will to men!"

At the altar rail the same figures swung about, still singing. They stood there, hand in hand, till the carol ended. There were many stanzas, and they sang them all. At the end they walked gravely down the aisle and seated themselves each in the other's place, while the people stared.

Little Lethia Cain nestled down beside Mrs. Drinkwater, and beamed up into her astonished face with a friendly smile.

"*He* would have—the Lord—you know," she whispered.

And across the aisle, in the Cain pew, little Gerry Drinkwater snuggled down comfortably, with an audible sigh of relief.

"I'm glad *that's* over!" he whispered distinctly. "We did it 'cause 'twas Christmas, and *He'd* have liked to hear us singin' out of the same hymnbook, you know. That's why we've swapped places, too—to make 'peace on earth.' Don't you see?"

"Yes," whispered Mrs. Cain, softly, "I see, Gerry." And she glanced across at the other mother with a little of Gerry's "peace on earth" in her softened face.

* * * * *

The sermon in the orchard had borne its fruit. The other sermon on Christmas morning was to bear fruit too, for the young minister preached as never before, and his congregation listened. The little children had led them—should they not follow?

The lines of patient worry in Rebekah Taft's face smoothed out one by one. A presence of peace to come stole into her troubled heart and comforted it. Over the whole church brooded the Christmas spirit of love and peace and good fellowship.

And the minister did not resign.

"Meditation" in a Minor Key

Joe L. Wheeler

Can a person's life be dominated by a single piece of music? Two people's lives?

EIGHT minutes until curtain time, Mr. Devereaux."

"How's it looking?"

"Full house. No. *More* than full house—they're already turning away those who'll accept Standing Room Only tickets."

"Frankly, I'm a bit surprised, Mr. Schobel. My last concert here was not much of a success."

"I remember, sir. The house was barely a third full."

"Hmm. I wonder . . . uh . . . what do you suppose has made the difference?"

"Well, for one thing, sir, it's your first-ever Christmas concert. For another, people are regaining interest—that Deutsche Gramophone recording has all Europe talking. But pardon me, sir. I'd better let you get ready. Good luck, sir."

And he was gone.

* * * * *

No question about it, he mused as he bowed to acknowledge the applause, the venerable Opera House was indeed full. As always, his eyes panned the sea of faces as he vainly searched for the one who never came—had not in 10 long years. He had *so* hoped tonight would be different. That package—it hadn't done the job after all . . .

Ten years ago . . . tonight . . . it was. Right here in Old Vienna. It was to have been the happiest Christmas Eve in his life—was Ginevra not to become his bride the next day?

What a fairy-tale courtship that had been. It had all started at the Salzburg Music Festival, where he was the center of attention, not only of the city but of the world. Had he not stunned concert-goers by his incredible coup—the first pianist ever to win grand piano's Triple Crown: the Van Cliburn, the Queen Elizabeth, and the Tchaikovsky competitions?

Fame had built steadily as one after another of the great prizes had fallen to him. Now, as reporters, interviewers, and cameramen followed his every move, he grew drunk on the wine of adulation.

It began as he leaned over the parapet of Salzburg Castle, watching the morning sun gild the rooftops of the city below. He had risen early in order to hike up the hill to the castle and watch the sunrise. A cool alpine breeze ruffled the trees just above—but it also displaced a few strands of raven black hair only a few feet to his left. Their glances met—and they both glanced away, only to blush as they glanced back. She was the most beautiful girl he had ever seen. But beautiful in more than mere appearance: beautiful in poise and grace as well. Later, he would gradually discover her beauty of soul.

With uncharacteristic shyness, he introduced himself to her. And then she withdrew in confusion as she tied his name to the cover stories. Disarming her with a smile, he quickly changed the subject: what was *she* doing in Salzburg?

As it turned out, she was in Europe for a summer-long study tour—and how his heart leaped when she admitted that her study group was staying in Salzburg the entire week. He made the most of it—before her bus had moved on he had pried from her not very reluctant fingers a copy of the tour itinerary.

And like Jean Valjean's inexorable nemesis, Javert, he pursued her all over Europe, driving his concert manager into towering rages. Had he forgotten that there was the long and arduous fall schedule to prepare for? Had he forgotten the time it took to memorize a new repertoire? No, he hadn't forgotten. The truth of the matter was that his priorities had suddenly changed. Every midweek, in around-the-clock marathons, he'd given his practicing its due—

then he'd escape in order to be with Ginevra for the weekend.

They were instant soul mates. They both loved the mountains and the sea, dawn and dusk, Tolstoy and Twain, snow and sand, hiking and skiing, gothic cathedrals and medieval castles, sidewalk cafes and old bookstores. But they were not clones. In art, she loved Georges de la Tour and Caravaggio, whereas his patron saints were Dürer and Hieronymus Bosch; in music, he preferred Mozart and Prokofiev, whereas she reveled in Chopin and Liszt.

He knew the day he met her that, for him, there would never be another woman. He was that rarity, a man who out of the whole world will choose but one—and if that one be denied him . . .

But he wasn't denied. It was on the last day of her stay, just hours before she boarded her plane for home, that he asked her to climb with him the zig-zagging inner staircases of the bell tower of Votivkirche, that great neogothic cathedral of Vienna, paling in comparison only with its legendary ancestor, St. Stephens.

Far up in the tower, breathing hard for more than one reason, his voice shook as he took both her hands captive and looked through her honest eyes into her heart—his, he knew, even without asking. She never *did* actually say yes, for the adorable curl of her lips, coupled with the candlelit road to heaven in her eyes, was her undoing.

The rapture that followed comes only once in a lifetime—when it comes at all.

Then the scene changed . . . and he stiffened as if receiving a mortal blow . . . for but four months later, in that self-same bell tower, his world had come to an end. That terrible, terrible night when his nuptial dreams were slain by a violin.

* * * * *

Ginevra drew her heavy coat tighter around her as the airport limousine disappeared into the night. Inside the Opera House she made her way to the ticket counter to pick up her pre-reserved ticket.

From the other side of the doors she heard Bach's "Italian Concerto" being reborn. She listened intently. She had not been mistaken after all: a change *had* taken place.

Leaning against a pillar, she let the distant notes wash over her while she took the scroll of her life and unrolled a third of it. How vividly she remembered that memorable autumn. Michael's letters came as regularly as night following day: long letters most of the time, short messages when his hectic schedule precluded more. Her pattern was unvarying: she would walk up the mountain road to the mailbox and from the day's mail search for that precious envelope, then carry it unopened on top of the rest of the mail back to the chalet that perched high on a promontory point 1600 feet above the Denver plain. Then she'd walk out onto the upper deck and seat herself. Off to her right were the Flatirons massed above the city of Boulder. Front and center was the skyline of Denver—at night a fairyland of twinkling lights; to

the left, the mountains stair-stepped up to 14,255-foot Longs Peak and Rocky Mountain National Park. Next she'd listen for the pines—oh! those heavenly pines! They would be sighing their haunting song . . . and *then* she would open his letter.

So full of romance were her starlit eyes that weeks passed before she realized there was a hairline crack in her heart—and Michael was the cause of it. She hadn't realized it during that idyllic summer when the two of them had spent so much time exploring gothic cathedrals, gazing transfixed as light transformed stained-glass into heart-stopping glory, sitting on transepts as organists opened their stops and called on their pipes to dare the red zone of reverberating sound.

Finally, in a long letter, she asked him point-blank whether or not he believed in God. His response was a masterpiece of subterfuge and fence-straddling, for well he knew how central the Lord was to her. As women have since the dawn of time, she rationalized that if he just loved *her* enough—and surely he *did*—then of course he would come to love God as much as she.

So she put her reservations and premonitions aside, and deflected her parents' concerns in that respect as well. Michael had decided he wanted to be married in the same cathedral where he had proposed to her—and as it was large enough to accommodate family as well as key figures of the music world, she had reluctantly acquiesced. Personally, she much rather would have been married in the small Boulder church high up on Mapleton Avenue. A Christmas wedding there, in the church she so loved . . . But it was not to be.

Deciding to make the best of it, she and her family drove down the mountain, took the freeway to Stapleton Airport, boarded the plane, and found their seats. As the big United jet roared off the runway, she looked out the window at Denver and her beloved Colorado receding below her. She wondered, could Michael's European world ever really take its place?

It was cold that memorable Christmas Eve, and the snow lay several feet deep on Viennese streets. Ginevra, ever the romantic, shyly asked Michael if he would make a special pilgrimage with her.

"Where to?" queried Michael. "It's mighty cold outside."

"The bell tower of Votivkirche."

He grinned that boyish grin she loved. "I really *am* marrying a sentimentalist, aren't I? Oh, well," he complained good-naturedly, "I guess I'd better get used to it. Let's find our coats."

An unearthly quiet came over the great city as they once again climbed the winding staircases of Votivkirche. She caught her breath at the beauty of it all when they at last reached their aerie and looked down at the frosted rooftops and streets below. Michael, however, much preferred the vision she represented, in her flame-colored dress and sable coat.

Then it was . . . faintly and far away . . . that they heard it. They never did trace its origin exactly; it might have wafted its way up the tower from below, or it might have come from an apartment across the way. Ordinarily, in the cacophony of the city, they could not possibly have heard it, but tonight, with snow deadening the street sounds, they could distinctly pick up every note. Whoever the violinist was . . . was a master.

Ginevra listened, transfixed. Michael, noting her tear-stained cheeks, shattered the moment with an ill-timed laugh. "Why, you old crybaby. It's nothing but a song! I've heard it somewhere before. I don't remember who wrote it, but it's certainly nothing to cry over."

He checked as he saw her recoil as if he had slashed her face with a whip. Her face blanched, and she struggled for control. After a long pause she said in a toneless voice, "It is not a song . . . It is 'Meditation,' by Massenet."

"Well, that's fine with me," quipped Michael. "I'll just meditate about *you*."

There was a long silence, and now quite ill at ease, he shuffled his feet and tried to pass it all off as a joke.

But in that he failed abysmally. "You . . . you don't hear it at all," she cried. "You just don't . . . I never hear that melody without tears . . . or without soaring to heaven on the notes. Massenet had to have been a Christian! . . . And, furthermore, whoever plays it like we just heard it played *has* to be a Christian, too!"

"Oh, come now, Ginevra. Aren't you getting carried away by a simple little ditty? Anyone who really knows how to play the violin could play it just as well. *I certainly could*—and I don't even believe in . . . in God . . ." He stopped, vainly trying to slam his lips on the words in time, but perversely they slipped out of their own accord.

Deep within the citadel of her innermost being, Ginevra felt her heart shudder as if seized by two powerful opposing forces. Then, where once was the hairline crack of her heart, there was an awful "*crack*"—and a yawning chasm took its place.

The look of agony on her face brought him to his senses at last—but it was too late. She looked at him with glaciered cheeks and with eyes so frozen that he could barely discern the tiny flickering that had, only moments ago, almost overpowered him with the glow of a thousand lovelit candles.

She turned, slipped something that had been on her finger into his coat pocket, and was gone. So quickly was the act done that at first he failed to realize she was no longer there. Then he called after her and ran blindly down the stairs. Ginevra, however, with the instinct of a wounded animal, found an unlocked stairwell door and hid inside until he had raced down the tower and into the street. Much later, she silently made her way out into a world made glad by midnight bells—but there was no Christmas gladness in *her* heart.

She determined to never see him again. Neither his calls nor his letters nor his telegrams would she answer; she wrote him only once: "Please do not *ever* try to contact me in any way again."

And he, his pride in shreds, never had.

* * * * *

Never would he forget that awful Christmas when—alone—he had to face the several thousand wedding guests and the importunate press with the news that it was all off. No, he could give them no reasons—and then he had fled.

Since he had planned on an extended honeymoon he had no more concerts scheduled until the next fall. That winter and spring he spent much time in solitude, moping and feeling sorry for himself. By late spring he was stir-crazy—so he fled to the South Pacific, to Asia, to Africa, to South America—anywhere to get away from himself and his memories.

Somehow, by mid-summer he began to regain control; he returned to Europe and quickly mastered his fall repertoire. That fall, most of his reviews were of the rave variety, for he dazzled with his virtuosity and technique.

For several years, his successes continued—and audiences filled concert halls wherever he performed. But there came a day when that was no longer true, when he realized that most dreaded of performing world truths: that it was all over—he had peaked. Here he was, his career hardly begun . . . and his star was already setting. But *why?*

Reviewers and concert-goers alike tried vainly to diagnose the ailment and prescribe medicinal cures, but nothing worked. More and more the tenor of the reviews began to sound like the following:

"How sad it is that Devereaux, once thought to be the rising star of our age, the worthy successor to Horowitz, has been revealed as but human clay after all. It is as if he represents but a case of arrested development. Normally, as a pianist lives and ages, the roots sink deeper and the storm-battered trunk and branches develop seasoning and rugged strength. Not so with Devereaux. It's as if all growth ceased some time ago. Oh! No one can match him where it comes to razzle-dazzle and special effects, but one gets a bit tired of these when there is no offsetting depth."

Like a baseball slugger in a prolonged batting slump, Michael tried everything; he dabbled in every philosophy or mysticism he came across. Like a drunken bee, he reeled from hive to hive without any real sense of direction.

And "Meditation" had gradually become an obsession with him; he just couldn't seem to get it out of his consciousness. He determined to prove to her that one didn't have to be religious in order to play it well. But as much as he tried, as much as he applied his vaunted techniques and interpretive virtuosity to it, it yet remained as flat, stale, and unmoving as three-hour-old coffee.

He even went to the trouble of researching the tune's origins, feeling confident that it, like much music that concert performers play, would apparently have no religious connections whatsoever. In his research he discovered that "Meditation" came from Massenet's opera *Thais*, which he knew had to do with a dissolute courtesan. Aha! He had her! But then he dug deeper and discovered, to his chagrin, that although it was true that Thais had a dissolute sexual past, as was true with Mary Magdalene, she was redeemed—and "Meditation" represents the intermezzo bridge between the pagan past of the first two acts and the oneness with God in the third act.

So he had to acknowledge defeat here, too.

As for Ginevra, she was never far from his thoughts. But not once would his pride permit him to ask anyone about her, her career, or whether or not she had ever married.

He just *existed* . . . and measured his life by concerts and hotel rooms.

* * * * *

Ginevra too, after the numbness and shock had at last weathered into a reluctant peace, belatedly realized that life had to go on—but just what should she do with her life?

It was during a freak spring blizzard that snowed her in that the answer came. She had been sitting in the conversation pit of the massive three-story-high moss rock fireplace, gazing dreamily into the fire, when suddenly the mood came upon her to write. She reached for a piece of paper, picked up her Pilot pen, and began writing a poem. A poem about pain, disillusion, and heartbreak. The next day she mailed it off to a magazine and, not long after, it was published.

She decided to do graduate work in the humanities and in education. She completed a master's and later a Ph.D., in the process becoming the world's foremost authority on the life and times of a woman writer of the American heartland. She also continued, as her busy schedule permitted, to write poems, essays, short stories, inspirational literature, and longer works of fiction.

So it was that Ginevra became a teacher, a teacher of writing, of literature—and life. Each class was a microcosm of life itself; in each class were souls crying out to be ministered to, to be appreciated, to be loved.

Because of her charm, vivacity, joie de vivre, and sense of humor, she became ever more popular and beloved with the passing of the years. She attracted suitors like children to a toy store—yet, though some of these friendships got to the threshold of love, none of them got any further. It was as if every last one of them paled in comparison with what she had left behind in Vienna.

The good Lord it was who saw her through, who shored up her frailties and helped to mend the brokenness.

Meanwhile, she did find time to keep up with Michael's life and career. In doing so, she bought all his recordings, playing them often. Yet she was vaguely dissatisfied—she too noting the lack of growth—and wondered.

One balmy day in late November, during the seventh year after the breakup, as she was walking down the ridge to her home she stopped to listen to her two favorite sounds—the cascading creek cavorting its way down to the Front Range plain, and the sibilant whispering of the pines. Leaning against a large rock, she looked up at that incredibly blue sky of the Colorado high country.

As always, her thoughts refused to stay in their neat little cages. She had tried all kinds of locks during those seven years—but not one of them worked. And now, when she had thought them safely locked in, here came all her truant thoughts, bounding up to her like a rag-tag litter of exuberant puppies, overjoyed at finding her hiding place.

And every last one of the little mutts was yelping Michael's name.

What would *he* be doing this Christmas? It bothered her—had bothered her for almost seven years now—that her own judge had refused to acquit her for her Michael-related words and actions. Periodically, during these years, she had submitted her case to the judge in the courthouse of her mind; and every time, after listening to the evidence, the judge had looked at her stern-faced. She would bang the gavel on the judicial bench and intone severely: "Insufficient evidence on which to absolve you. . . . Next case?"

She couldn't get out of her head an article she had read several months before, an article about Michael Devereaux. The writer, who had interviewed her subject in depth, had done her homework well, for the portrait of Michael rang true to Ginevra. The individual revealed in the character sketch was both the Michael Ginevra knew and a Michael she would rather not know. The interviewer pointed out that Michael was a rather bitter man for one so young in years. So skittish had the interviewee been, whenever approached on the subject of women in his life, that the writer postulated as her personal conviction that somewhere along the way Devereaux had been terribly hurt by someone he loved deeply. . . . And here, Ginevra winced.

The writer concluded her character portrait with a disturbing synthesis: "Devereaux, his concert career floundering, appears to be searching for answers. But he's not looking in the direction of God. Like many, if not most, Europeans of our time, he appears to be almost totally secular; thus he has nowhere but within himself upon which to draw strength and inspiration. Sadly, his inner wells appear to retain only shallow reservoirs from which to draw. A pity."

A nagging thought returned to tug at her heartstrings: What had *she* done—what had she *ever* done—to show Michael a better way?

"But," she retorted, "I don't want him to become a Christian just for *me!*" But this time that oft-used cop-out didn't suffice; she kept seeing that stern-faced judge within. In the long, long silence that followed was born a plan of action. If it worked, if he responded as she hoped he might . . . sooner or later . . . she would *know!* For inescapably, the secret would "out" through his music.

She determined to implement her plan of action that very day.

114

Several weeks after Ginevra's decision, Michael had returned to his hotel after a concert, a particularly unsatisfactory one—and it seemed these days that there were more and more of this kind. Even the crowd had been smaller than any he could remember in years. He was convinced that his career and life were both failures—and that there was little reason to remain living. He went to bed and vainly tried to sleep. After an hour or two of thrashing around, he got up, turned on the light, and looked for the last packet of mail forwarded to him by his agent. There was something in it that intrigued him. Ah! Here it was.

A small registered package had arrived via air mail from New York. There was no return address, and he didn't recognize the handwriting on the mailer. Inside was a slim, evidently long-out-of-print book titled *The Other Wise Man*, written by an author he had never heard of—Henry Van Dyke. Well, it looked like a quick read and he couldn't sleep anyhow . . .

A quick read it was not—he found himself rereading certain passages several times. It was after 3:00 a.m. before he finally put it down. He was moved in spite of himself. Then he retired, this time to sleep.

During that Christmas season, he reread it twice more, and each time he read it he wondered what had motivated that unknown person to send it.

Three months later came another registered packet from New York. It too was obviously a book and, to his joy, another old one. To his relief—for he had an intense fear of God and religion—it did not appear to be a religious book. The author and title were alike unknown to him: Myrtle Reed's *The Master's Violin*. The exquisite metallic lamination of this turn-of-the-century first edition quite took his breath away. *Someone* had spent some money on *this* gift! He read it that night, and it seemed, in some respects, that the joy and pain he vicariously experienced in the reading mirrored his own. And the violin! It brought back memories of that melody, that melody that just would not let him go, that melody that represented the high tide of his life.

It was mid-June, three months later, when the next registered package arrived from New York. This time, his hands were actually trembling as he opened the package. Another book by yet another author he had never heard of: Harold Bell Wright. Kind of a strange title it had: *That Printer of Udel's*. But it was old and had a tipped-in cover; the combination was irresistible. He dropped everything and started to read.

He was not able to put it down. In it he saw depicted a portrait of Christian living unlike any he had ever seen before—a way of life that had to do not just with sterile doctrine but with a living, loving outreach to one's fellowman. He finished the book late that night. A month later, he read it again.

By late September, he had been watching his mail with great anticipation for some time. What would it be this time? Then it came, another book, first published in 1907, by the same author as the last one, with the intriguing title *The Calling of Dan Matthews*. It made the same impact upon him that its predecessor had.

Nevertheless, Michael was no easy nut to crack: he continued to keep his jury sequestered—he was nowhere near ready for a verdict of any kind.

Early in December arrived his second Van Dyke: *The Mansion*, a lovely, lime-green, illustrated edition. This book spawned some exceedingly disturbing questions about his inner motivations. Of what value, really, was *his* life? When was the last time he had ever done anything for someone without expecting something in return? For such a small book, it certainly stirred up some difficult-to-answer questions!

March brought a book he had often talked about reading but never had the temerity to tackle, Victor Hugo's forbidding *Les Miserables*, almost 1,500 pages unabridged! He wondered, *Why?* Why such a literary classic following what he had been sent before? He didn't wonder long; the story of Jean Valjean was a story of redemption, the story of a man who climbed out of hell—the first Christ-figure he could ever remember seeing in French literature. By now, Michael was beginning to look for fictional characters who exhibited, in some manner, Christian values.

At the end of the book was a brief note:
"No other book for six months. Review."
He did . . . but he felt terribly abused, sorely

missing the expected package in June.

By the time September's leaves began to fall, he was in a state of intense longing. Certainly, after *Les Miserables*, and after a half-year wait, it would have to be a blockbuster! To his amazement and disgust, it was a slim mass-market paperback with the thoroughly unappetizing title of *Mere Christianity*. The author he had heard of but had never read—C. S. Lewis.

Swallowing his negative feelings with great difficulty, he gingerly tested with his toes . . . Lewis's "Jordan River." As he stepped further in, he was—quite literally—overwhelmed. Every argument he had ever thrown up as a barrier between himself and God was systematically and thoroughly demolished. He had had no idea that God and Christianity were any more than an amalgamation of feelings—for the first time, he was able to conceptualize God with his *mind!*

Whoever was sending him the books was either feeling sorry for making him wait so long—or punishing him by literally burying him in print! He was kindly given two weeks to digest *Mere Christianity* and then began the non-stop barrage of his soul: first came three shells in a row: Lewis's Space Trilogy, *Out of That Silent Planet*, *Perelandra*, and *That Hideous Strength*. At first, Michael, like so many other readers of the books, enjoyed the plot solely on the science fiction level—*then* he wryly observed to himself that Lewis had set him up: woven into the story was God and His plan of salvation!

The trilogy was followed by Lewis's *Screwtape Letters*. How Michael laughed as he read this one! How incredibly wily is the Great Antagonist! And how slyly Lewis had reversed the roles in order to shake up all his simplistic assumptions about the battles between Good and Evil.

A week later, another shell—*The Four Loves*. In it, Michael found himself reevaluating almost all of his people-related friendships in life. That was but the beginning. Then Lewis challenged him to explore the possibilities of a friendship with the Eternal.

Two shells then came in succession: *Surprised by Joy* and *A Grief Observed*. At long last, he was able to learn more about Lewis the man. Not only that, but how Lewis, so late in life introduced to the joys of nuptial love, related to the untimely death of his bride. How Lewis, in his wracking grief, almost lost his way—almost turned away God Himself! Parallelling Lewis's searing loss of his beloved was Michael's loss of Ginevra. Relived once again, it was bone-wrenching in its intensity. More so than Lewis's, for he had not Lewis's God to turn to in the darkest hour.

The final seven shells came in the form of what appeared to be, at first glance, a series of books for children: Lewis's *Chronicles of Narnia*. It took Michael some time to figure out why he had been sent this series last—after such heavy-weights! About half way through, he was, before he knew. By then, he had fully realized just how powerful a manifestation of the attributes of Christ was Aslan the lion. By the moving conclusion of *The Last Battle*, the 15 shells from Lewis's howitzer had made utter rubble out of Michael's defense system.

Then came a beautiful edition of the *Phillips Translation of the New Testament*. On the fly leaf, in neat black calligraphy, was this line: "May this book help to make your new year truly new."

He read the New Testament with a receptive attitude, taking a month to complete it. One morning, following a concert in Florence, he rose very early and walked to the Arno River to watch the sunrise. As he leaned against a lamp post, his thoughts (donning their accountant coats) did an audit of the past three years.

He was belatedly discovering that a life without God just wasn't worth living. In fact, *nothing*, he now concluded, had any lasting meaning divorced from a higher power. He looked around him, mentally scrutinizing the lives of family members, friends, and colleagues in the music world. He noted the devastating divorce statistics, the splintered homes, and the resulting flotsam of loneliness and despair. Without God, no human relationship was likely to last very long.

Nevertheless, even now that he was thoroughly convinced—in theory—that God represented the only way out of his dead-end existence, he bullheadedly balked at crossing the line out of the Dark into the Light.

The day before Easter of that tenth year, there came another old book, an expensive English first edition of Francis Thompson's poems. Inside, on the endsheet, was this coda to their faceless three-year friendship:

Dear Michael,
For almost three years now,
you have never been out of my
thoughts and prayers.
I hope that these books have come
to mean to you what they do to me.
This is your last book.
Please read "The Hound of Heaven."
The rest is up to you.
        Your Friend

Immediately, he turned to the long poem and immersed himself in Thompson's lines. Although some of the words were a bit antiquated and jarred a little, he felt that the lines were written laser-straight to him, especially these near the poem's gripping conclusion—for Michael identified totally with Thompson's own epic flight from the pursuing celestial Hound:

Whom will you find to love ignoble thee
    Save Me, save only Me?
All which I took from thee I did but take,
    Not for thy harms,
But just that thou might'st seek it in My arms.
    All which thy child's mistake
Fancies as lost, I have stored for thee at home.
    Rise, clasp My hand, and come!
These lines broke him, and he fell to his knees.

* * * * *

It was the morning after, and Michael awakened to the first Easter of the rest of his life. Needing very much to be alone, he decided to head for the family chalet near Mt. Blanc. How fortunate, he mused, that the rest of the family was skiing at St. Moritz this week.

Two hours before he got there, it began to snow, but his Porsche, itself born during a bitterly cold German winter, growled its delight as it devoured the road to Chamonix. It was snowing even harder when they arrived at the chalet, where Michael was greeted with delight by Jacques and Marie, the caretakers.

Breakfast was served adjacent to a roaring fire in the great alpine fireplace. Afterward, thoroughly satisfied, he leaned back in his favorite chair and looked out at the vista of falling snow.

He felt, he finally concluded, as if sometime in the night he had been reborn. It was as if all his life he had been carrying a staggeringly heavy backpack, a backpack into which some cruel overseer had dropped yet another five-pound brick, each January 1 of his life, for as far back as he could remember. And now, suddenly, he was *free!* What a paradoxical revelation that was, that the long-feared surrender to God resulted in, not dreaded strait-jacketed servitude, but the most incredible euphoric freedom he had ever imagined!

Looking back at the years of his life, he now recognized that he had been fighting God every step of the way. But God, refusing to give up on him, had merely kept His distance. He went to his suitcase, reached for that already precious book of poems, returned to his seat by the fire, and turned again to that riveting first stanza:

> I fled Him, down the nights and down the days;
> > I fled Him, down the arches of the years;
> I fled Him, down the labyrinthine ways
> > Of my own mind, and in the midst of tears
> I hid from Him, and under running laughter.
> > Up vistaed hopes I sped;
> > And shot, precipitated
> Adown Titanic glooms of chastened fears,
> > From those strong Feet that followed, followed
> > after.
> But with unhurrying chase,
> > And unperturbed pace,
> Deliberate speed, majestic instancy,
> > They beat—and a Voice beat
> > More instant than the Feet—
> "All things betray thee, who betrayest Me!"

He turned away, unable, because of a blurring of his vision, to read on. "How many *years* I have lost!" he sighed.

Years during which the frenetic pace of his life caused the Pursuing Hound to sadly drop back. Years during which he proudly strutted, wearing the tinsel crown of popularity. And then that flimsy bit of ephemera was taken away and the long descent into the maelstrom had taken place. And it had been in his darkest hour, when he actually felt

Ultimate Night reaching for him, that he plainly and distinctly heard his pursuer again.

For almost three years now that Pursuer had drawn ever closer. There had been a strange meshing—the Voice in the crucifixion earthquake who spoke to Artaban; the Power that defied the Ally in the Dan Matthews story; the Force revealed through the pulsating strings of "mine Cremona"; the Presence that, through the Bishop's incredible act of forgiveness and compassion, saved the shackled life of Jean Valjean; the Angel who showed John Weightman's pitiful mansion to him; Malacandra of the Perelandra story and Aslan in the Narnia series. As he read "The Hound of Heaven," all the foregoing lost their distinctiveness and merged into the pursuing Hound—they were one and the same!

* * * * *

Michael resonated with a strange new power, a power he had never experienced before—it was as if, during the night, in his badly-crippled power station (a generating facility to which, over the years, one incoming line after another had been cut, until he was reduced to but one frail piece of frayed wire that alone kept him from blackout), a new cable, with the capacity to illuminate an entire world, had been snaked down the dusty stairs, and then *plugged in.*

Then, from far back (even before his descent into hell), two images emerged out of the mists of time, one visual and one aural—the tear-stained face of the Only Woman, and the throbbing notes of "Meditation."

Tingling all over, he stood up and walked over to the grand piano always kept in the lodge for his practicing needs. He lifted the lid, seated himself on the bench, and looked up. Humbly, he asked the question: "Am I ready at last, Lord?"

Then he reached for the keys and began to play. As his fingers swept back and forth, something else occurred: for the first time in more than nine years he was able, without printed music, to replay in his mind every note he and Ginevra had heard in that far-off bell tower of Votivkirche. Not only that, but the sterility was gone! The current that had been turned on inside him leaped to his hands and fingers.

At last he was ready.

* * * * *

Michael immediately discarded the fall concert repertoire, chosen as it had been merely for showmanship reasons, and substituted a new musical menu. Ever so carefully, as a master chef prepares a banquet for royalty, he selected his individual items. In fact, he agonized over them, for each number must not only mesh with all the others but enhance as well, gradually building into a crescendo that would trumpet a musical vision of his new life.

Much more complicated was the matter of his new recording. How could he stop the process at such a late date? Not surprisingly, when he met with Polygram management and dropped his bombshell, they were furious. Only with much effort was he able to calm them down, and that on a premise they strongly doubted—that his replacement would be so much better, they would be more than compensated for the expected production expense!

He walked out of their offices in a very subdued mood. If he had retained any illusions about how low his musical stock had sunk, that meeting would have graphically settled the question. If his new recording failed to sell well, he would almost certainly be dropped from the label.

Then he memorized all the numbers before making his trial run recording. This way, he was able to give his undivided attention to interpretation before wrapping up the process. Only after he himself was thoroughly satisfied with the results did he have it recorded and then hand-carried by his agent to Deutsche Gramophone/Polygram management.

He didn't have to wait very long; only minutes after they played his pilot recording, Michael received a long-distance phone call from the president himself. Michael had known him for years and knew him to be a very tough hombre indeed. Recognizing full well that he and the company lived and died by the bottom line, he was used to making decisions for the most pragmatic of reasons. Recording artists feared him because he had a way of telling the unvarnished truth sans embellishments or grace-notes . . . And now he was on the line.

Initially almost speechless, the president finally recovered and blurted out, "What has happened, Michael? For years now, your recordings have seemed—pardon my candidness, but you know me—a bit tinny, fluffy, sometimes listless, and even a bit . . . uh . . . for want of a better word, peevish; more or less as if you were irritably going through the motions but with little idea why. . . . Now, here, on the other hand, comes a recording that sounded to us like you woke up one morning and decided to belatedly take control of your life and career; that there were new and exciting ways of interpreting music—with power . . . and beauty . . . and, I might add, Michael, a promise of depth and seasoning we quite frankly no longer believed was in you! *What has happened?*"

* * * * *

That incredible summer passed in a blur of activity. The long ebb over at last, the incoming tidal forces of Michael's life thundered up the beaches of the musical world. Deutsche Gramophone management and employees worked around the clock to process, release, and then market what they firmly believed would be the greatest recording of his career. Word leaked out even before it was released; consequently, there was a run on it when it hit the market. All of this translated into enthusiastic interest in his fall concert schedule.

Early in August, before the recording had been released, Michael phoned his New York agent, who could hardly contain himself about the new bookings that were flooding in for the North American tour in the spring of the following year. Michael, after first swearing him to secrecy, told him that he was entrusting to his care the most delicate assignment of their long association—one which, if botched, would result in irreparable damage. The agent promised.

He wanted of him three things: to trace the whereabouts of a certain lady (taking great pains to ensure that the lady in question would not be aware of the search process); to find out if the lady had married; to process a mailing, the contents of the mailing of which would be adjusted according to whether the lady had married or not.

* * * * *

Meanwhile, Ginevra played the waiting game—a very hard game to play without great frustration. For her, the frustration level had been steadily building for almost three years. *When* would she know?

Within a year after mailing her first book, she felt reasonably confident that he was reading what she had sent (at least partly, on the basis that none had been returned). But she had little data upon which to base her assumptions. During the second year, little snips of information relating to possible change in Devereaux appeared here and there. Nothing really significant, really, but enough to give her hope.

She had knelt down by her bed that memorable morning before she mailed Thompson's poems. In her heart-felt supplication, she reminded God that, with this book, she had now done all that was in her power to do. The rest was up to Him. Then she drove down the mountain to the Boulder post office and sent it to her New York relayer—and returned home to wait.

It was several months before the Devereaux-related excitement in the music world began to build. Her heart beat a lilting "allegro" the day she first heard about the growing interest in Michael's new recording—she could hardly wait to get a copy.

Then came the day when, in her mailbox, there was a little yellow piece of paper indicating that a registered piece of mail was waiting for her in the post office. It turned out to be a very large package from an unknown source in New York.

Not until she had returned to her chalet did she open it. Initially, she was almost certain that one of her former students was playing a joke on her, for the box was disproportionately light. She quickly discovered the reason—it was jammed full with wadded-up paper. Her room was half full of paper before she discovered the strange-shaped box at the very bottom of the mailing carton. *What* could it be? *Who* could it be from?

In this box, obviously packed with great care, were three items, each separated by a hard cardboard divider: a perfect flame-red rose in a sealed moisture-tight container, Michael's new Deutsche Gramophone recording, and an advance copy of a concert program, which read as follows:

**MICHAEL DEVEREAUX
FIRST CHRISTMAS EVE CONCERT**

VIENNA OPERA HOUSE

. . . followed by the other data giving exact time and date, as well as the program itself.

* * * * *

Fearing lest someone in the Standing section take her place, during the enthusiastic applause following Bach's "Italian Concerto" Ginevra asked an usher to escort her to her seat in the third row. Michael, who had turned to acknowledge the applause, caught the motion — the beautiful woman coming down the aisle. And she was wearing a flame-red rose. Even in Vienna, a city known for its beautiful women, she was a sight to pin dreams on.

How terribly grateful he was to the audience for continuing to clap, for that gave him time — precious time — in which to restore his badly damaged equilibrium. It was passing strange, mused Michael. For years now, both his greatest dream and his greatest nightmare were one and the same: that Ginevra would actually show up for one of his concerts. The nightmare had to do with deep-seated fear that her presence in the audience would inevitably destroy his concentration, and with it the concert itself. And now, here she was! If he ever needed a higher power, he needed it now. Briefly, he bowed his head. When he raised it, he felt again the new sense of serenity, peace, and command.

Leaving the baroque world of Bach, he turned to César Franck; being a composer of romantic music, but with baroque connections, he seemed to Michael to be a perfect bridge from Bach to Martin and Prokofiev. As he began to play Franck's "Prelude: Chorale et Fugue," he settled down to making this the greatest concert of his career. He had sometimes envied the great ones their announced conviction that, for each, the greatest concert was always the very next one on the schedule — they *never* took a free ride on their laurels. Only this season had he joined the masters, belatedly recognizing that the greatest thanks he could ever give his Maker would be to extend his powers to the limits, every time he performed, regardless of how large or how small the crowd.

The Opera House audience quickly recognized the almost mind-boggling change in attitude. The last time he had played here, reviewers had unkindly but accurately declared him washed up. So desperate for success of any kind had he become that he openly pandered to what few people still came. It was really pathetic; he would edge out onto the platform like an abused puppy, cringing lest he be kicked again. Not surprisingly, what he apparently expected, he got.

Now, there was no question as to who was in control. On the second, he would stride purposefully onto the stage, with a pleasant look on his face, and gracefully bow. He would often change his attire between sections; that added a visual extra to the auditory. His attire was always impeccable; newly cleaned and pressed, he was neither over nor underdressed for the occasion.

But neither was he proud, recognizing just how fragile is the line between success and failure—and how terribly difficult it is to stay at the top once you get there. Nor did he anymore grovel or play to the galleries. The attitude he now projected was, quite simply: "I'm so pleased you honored me by coming out tonight. I have prepared long and hard for this occasion; consequently, it is both my intent and my expectation that we shall share the greatest musical hour and a half of our lifetimes."

Ginevra felt herself becoming part of a living, breathing island in time. Every concert performed well, is that—sort of a magic moment during which outside life temporarily ceases to be. Great music is, after all, outside of time and thus not subject to its rules. Thus Ginevra, like the Viennese audience, lost all sense of identify, as Devereaux's playing became all the reality they were to know for some time.

These weren't just notes pried from a reluctant piano that they were hearing: this was life itself, life with all its frustrations and complexities.

With such power and conviction did César Franck speak from the grave that they stood applauding for three minutes at the end of the first half. In fact, disregarding Opera House protocol, a number of the younger members of the audience swarmed onto the stage and surrounded Michael before he could retire. The new Michael stopped, and with a pleasant look on his face all the while, autographed every program that was shoved at him. Nay, more than that; as one of these autograph seekers, jubilant of face, came back to Ginevra's row, she saw him proudly showing the program to his parents. Michael had taken the trouble to learn each person's name so that he could inscribe each one personally!

Michael's tux was wringing wet. As for the gleaming black Boersendorfer, with such superhuman energy had Michael attacked it that it begged for the soothing balm of a piano tuner's ministrations; hence it was wheeled out for a badly needed rest. In its place was the monarch of the city's Steinway grands. Michael had specifically requested this living nine feet of history. No one knew for sure just how old it was, but it had for years been the pride and joy of Horowitz. Rubinstein would play here on no other, and it was even rumored that the great Paderewski performed on it.

Michael, like all real artists, deeply loved his favorite instruments. Like the fabled Velveteen Rabbit, when an instrument such as this Steinway has brought so much happiness, fulfillment, meaning, and love into life . . . well, over the years, it ceases to be just a piano and approaches personhood. Thus it was that Michael, before it was wheeled in, had a heart-to-heart chat with it.

A stage hand, watching the scene, didn't even lift an eyebrow—concert musicians were all a loony bunch.

* * * * *

Only after a great deal of soul searching had Michael decided to open the second half of his concert with Swiss-born Frank Martin's "Eight Preludes." He had long appreciated and loved Martin's fresh approach to music, his lyrical euphonies. Martin reminded Michael of the American composer Howard Hanson—he often had a difficult time choosing which one to include in a given repertoire. But this season, it was Martin's turn.

More and more sure of himself, Michael only gained in power as he retold Martin's story; by the time he finished the Preludes he owned Vienna. The deafening applause rolled on and on; nobody appeared willing to ever sit down.

Finally, the house quiet once again, a microphone was brought out and Michael stepped up to speak.

"Ladies and gentlemen," he began, "I have a substitution to make. As you know, I am scheduled to perform Prokofiev's 'Sonata No. 6 in A Major, Opus 82' as my concluding number. But I hope you will not be *too* disappointed"—and here he smiled his boyish grin—"if I substitute a piece that I composed, a piece that has never before been performed in public."

He paused, then continued: "Ten years ago tonight, in this fair city, this piece of music was born. But it was not completed until late this spring; I have been saving it for tonight." And here he dared to glance in the direction of Ginevra.

"The title is . . . 'Variations on a Theme by Massenet.' "

* * * * *

Nothing in Michael's composing experience had been more difficult than deciding what to do with "Meditation." Nor did the difficulties fall away with his conversion. He still had some tough decisions to face: Should his variations consist merely as creative side-trips from that one melodic base? By doing so, he knew he could dazzle. Should the variations be limited to musical proof that he and his Maker were now friends? With neither was he satisfied.

Of all the epiphanies he had ever experienced, none could compare with the one that was born to him one "God's in His heaven / All's right with the world" spring morning, a realization that he could create a counterpart to what Massenet had done with the "Meditation" intermezzo—a fusion of earthly love with the divine. Belatedly, he recognized a great truth: God does not come to us in the abstract; He comes to us through flesh and blood. We do not initially fall in love with God as a principle; rather, we first fall in love with human beings whose lives radiate friendship with the divine. It is only then that we seek out God on our own.

Ginevra was such a prototype—that is why he had fallen in love with her. And he had little doubt in his mind but that it was she who had choreographed his conversion. No one else had he ever known who would have cared enough to institute and carry out such a flawless plan of action. Besides, some of the book choices made him mighty suspicious.

Michael had also recognized what all true artists do sooner or later, that their greatest work must come from within, from known experience. If he was to endow his variations with power akin to the original, they must emanate from the joys and sorrows that made him what he was . . . and since she and God were inextricably woven together in Michael's multi-hued bolt of life, then woven together they must remain throughout the composition.

It would not be acceptable for her to distance herself and pretend she could judge what he had become dispassionately. No, Ginevra must enter into the world he had composed . . . and decide at the other end whether or not she would stay.

* * * * *

In Ginevra's mind, everything seemed to harken back to that cold night in the tower of Votivkirche, for it was there that two lives, only hours from oneness, had seen the cable of their intertwining selves unravel in only seconds.

Furthermore, there was more than God holding them apart, more than her romanticism as compared to Michael's realism. That far-off exchange of words had highlighted for her some significant problems that, left unresolved, would preclude marriage even if Michael had been converted. Let's see; how could she conceptualize them?

Essentially, it all came down to these: Michael had laughed at and ridiculed her deepest-felt feelings. Had made light of her tears. Had shown a complete absence of empathy. Worse yet, he exhibited a clear-cut absence of the one most crucial character trait in the universe—*kindness*. Also, at no time since she had known him had she ever seen him admit in any way that he was wrong about anything—and compounding the problem, he had refused to disclose his true identity to her: There had been a locked door half-way down to his heart. There had been another locked door half-way up to his soul. As far as she knew, both doors were still closed. But if they ever were to be unlocked . . . "Meditation" would be the key.

* * * * *

Finale

As-soft-as-a-mother's-touch pianissimo, Michael begins to play. So softly that there appears to be no breaks at all between the notes, but rather a continuous skein of melodic sound. And, for the first time in Michael's career, there is a flowing oneness with the piano—impossible to tell where flesh, blood, and breath end and where wood, ivory, and metal join.

Ginevra cannot help but feel tense in spite of blurred fingers weaving dreams around her. Deep down, she knows that what occurs during this piece of music will have a profound effect upon the rest of her life. And the rest of Michael's life.

But she hadn't traveled 5,000 miles just to be a referee or a critic. If their two worlds were ever to be one, she must leave her safe seat in the audience and step into the world of Michael's composition. Strangely enough—and living proof that it is the "small" things in life that are often the most significant—Michael's exhibition of kindness to the young people who blocked his exit during intermission strongly predisposes her in his favor.

How beautifully his arpeggios flow, cascading as serenely as alpine brooks singing their way down to the sea. All nature appears to be at peace. As Michael plays, she can envision the birds' wake-up calls, the falling rain and drifting snow, the sighing of her dear pines, and the endless journey of the stars. The world is a beautiful place . . . and love is in the air.

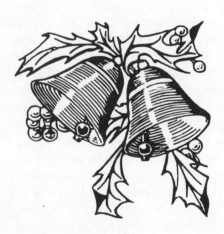

Suddenly, she stiffens. Certainly those are bells she is hearing. Yes—Christmas bells, flooding the universe with joy. She listens intently as their pealing grows ever louder—then *that theme!* It begins to mesh with the bells, but only for an instant. Right in the middle of it there is an ominous shift from major to minor key, and from harmony to dissonance. And the bells! In that self-same instant the pealing joy ceases and is replaced by tolling sorrow. How uncannily perfect is Michael's capture of that moment, that moment when all the joy in their world went sour.

The dissonance and tolling eventually give way to a classical music potpourri. Here and there she recognizes snatches of well-known themes, some of them from piano concertos. But the notes are clipped off short and played perfunctorily, more or less as if the pianist doesn't much care how they sound as long as they all get played in record time. Several times, the Theme tries to edge in . . . but each time it is rudely repulsed.

Now Dvorak's "New World Symphony" thunders in. Aha! At last, some resolution! Some affirmation! Not so; it quickly becomes apparent that this paean to a brave new world is, ironically, in steady retreat instead of advancing to triumph. Almost—it seems to her—as if it were a retrograde "Bolero," its theme progressively diminishing in power instead of increasing. Once again, "Meditation" seeks entry; once again, it is unceremoniously disposed of.

By now, Ginevra is deciphering Michael's musical code quite well: vividly revealed has been the progressive deterioration of Michael both as a person and as a pianist. From the moment in the cathedral tower when the bells began to toll, every variation that followed has dealt with the stages of his fall.

Then, clouds close in, thunder rumbles in the east, lightning strikes short-circuit the sky—and the rain falls. Torrents of it. Darkness sweeps in, and with it all the hells loose on this turbulent planet. Ginevra shivers as Michael stays in minor keys, mourning all the sadness and pain in the universe.

The winds gradually increase to hurricane strength. Far ahead of her—for she is exposed to the elements, too—she sees Michael, almost out of sight in the gloom, retreating from the storm. She follows, and attempts to call to him, but to no avail; the tempest swallows the words before they can be formed. Then the black clouds close in . . . and she loses sight of him altogether.

As the hurricane reaches ultimate strength, major keys are in full flight from the minors (Ginevra had discovered some time back that Michael is equating majors with the forces of Light, and minors with the forces of Darkness). It does not seem possible that any force on earth could save Michael from destruction.

It is now, in the darkest midnight, when the few majors left are making their last stand—and she senses that, for Michael, the end is near; now, when she has all but conceded victory to the Dark Power— that she again hears the strains of Thais' theme! How can such a frail thing possibly survive when leagued against the legions of Darkness? But . . . almost unbelievably . . . it does.

At this instant, Ginevra chances to look with wide-open eyes at, not Michael the pianist, but Michael the man. He has clearly forgotten all about the world, the concert audience, even *her*. In his total identification with the struggle for his soul, he is playing for only two people: himself—the penitent sinner—and God. And his face? Well, never afterward could she really explain, but one thing was absolutely certain—there before her . . . was Michael's naked soul.

With Michael's surrender, the tide turns at last; the storm rages on, but the enemy is now unmistakably in retreat. Dissonance and minors contest every step of the battlefield, trying vainly to hold off the invading Light. Then victorious majors begin sweeping the field.

Ginevra discovers in all this a great truth: It is minors that reveal the full beauty of majors. Had she not heard "Meditation" sobbing on the ropes of a minor key, she would never have realized the limitless power of God. It is the minor key that gives texture and beauty to the major, and it is dissonance that, by contrast, reveals the glory of harmony. It is sorrow that brings our wandering feet back to God.

Finally, with the mists beginning to dissipate and the sun breaking through, the Theme reappears, but alone for the first time. Now it is that Ginevra feels the full upward surge of the music . . . for "Meditation" soars heavenward with such passion, pathos, and power that gravity is powerless to restrain it.

And Ginevra . . . her choice made . . . reaches up, and with Michael,

climbs the stairs of heaven to God.

Dedication

This story is dedicated to my dearly beloved brother Romayne, who himself is a living embodiment of all that is finest in the concert piano profession—and who has lived in, and loved, Vienna for almost a third of a century now. As for Votivkirche, just months ago my daughter Michelle climbed that self-same bell tower with her Uncle Romayne, who performs in that cathedral every summer.

How This Story Came to Be

For as far back as I can remember, I have been haunted by "Meditation"—every time I hear it, I cry. It has moved me as no other piece of music in my lifetime. It was while listening to Zamfir's pan flute rendition of it that the dream for this story was born.

For a long time, I have wanted to articulate in story form a music-related narrative much like this, but until now lacked the vehicle, the glue that would hold the story together. All this, Massenet's "Meditation" provided.

After having sketched out the story line, I let it germinate for several months. Up till that time, I knew nothing of "Meditation's" origins except its authorship. It was at this juncture that I brought in Ingrid Vargas, of Takoma Park, Maryland—herself a pianist and organist, and one of my dear soul sisters. I sketched out the story line to her and asked if she would collaborate with me. She agreed to do some research on the work's origins. I'll admit I was mighty apprehensive: What if the piece proved—as was more than likely—to have no religious tie-ins at all; worse yet, had its roots in the opposite camp?

I'll never forget the day Ms. Vargas came bursting into my office, in great excitement exclaiming: "You were *right!*" Upon getting her calmed down, she showed me the results of her research: the piece was composed as a bridge between the secular and spiritual realms of our lives.

Additionally, Ms. Vargas has helped me with the concert program itself—no small endeavor!—as well as helping me each step of the way so that the musical authenticity would be there. (Even though I know the concert world fairly well, having directed a concert-stage series for 10 years, I needed additional musical expertise.) She is the only person to hear the completed story before the final copy. So, in a very special sense, this is her story, too.